Praise for *Hosts*

A glorious collection of stories, cause for celebration and gratitude. The final one, *Providence*, gestures toward all the others, suggesting the hidden design lying just beneath the surface of our lives connecting us all. Stories of children, of wounded veterans and lonely widows, of gay men and remembered blue roses painted on a ceiling. Of parasites and paradise. But the story I hope never to forget is called "Kick" and must have been written at the dictation of the gods. All honor.　　　　　　　　　　　　　　　　—KATHLEEN HILL

Alfred Corn's stories are just as elegant, complex, and perceptive as are his poems, full of surprises and passages of melancholy and yearning that recall the great short-fiction boom of the 1950s and 1960s. What a pleasure to read such a rewarding and sophisticated collection.　　　　　—RICK MOODY

Alfred Corn has an eye, and he uses his acute vison to great effect, an ability to make the reader aware of a whole world, and, too, the wonder of being aware, which luminous wonder is the pleasure of these stories. Having read a story by Alfred Corn, I look about at all that is around me for being suddenly magically there.　　　　　　　　　　　　　　　　　—DAVID PLANTE

Praise for *Part of His Story*

Given his interest in the nature and extent of human relationships, it is no surprise that Corn has at last written a novel, the title of which—*Part of His Story*—registers his sense that literary representation, whether in a novel or a poem, exists in a state of incompleteness…. [Corn] aims for something other than conventional realism: This novel is true to life in its scope and rhythm as well as in its characters and events.　　　　　—A. O. SCOTT, *The Nation*

HOSTS
Stories

HOSTS
Stories

Alfred Corn

MADHAT PRESS
CHESHIRE, MASSACHUSETTS

MadHat Press
MadHat Incorporated
PO Box 422, Cheshire, MA 01225

ISBN 978-1-968422-04-2 (paperback)

The Library of Congress has assigned
this edition a Control Number of
2025951348

Words by Alfred Corn
Cover art: *Le Chemin* by Albert Gleizes, 1911
Cover design by Marc Vincenz
Book design by MadHat Press

www.madhat-press.com

First Printing
Printed in the United States of America

Table of Contents

COUNTRY HOSTS

Adults are a mysterious race, and when they are our parents, nearly impossible to fathom. We almost never questioned their whims; whoever did that risked a formulaic "because I told you so," which bruised the part of the mind that relies on a reasonable sense of cause and effect. Many of the decisions they made for us had a quality much like other afflictions from on high—lightning bolts, earthquakes, plagues. When events are irrational and incredible, they seem divinely foreordained.

Not that there was anything especially dire about the plans made for me that summer. Maybe it was odd that my sisters weren't coming with me, but still the prospect of a month spent on my mother's cousin's farm sounded like an *adventure*, and adventure ranks high with ten-year-olds. I'd been there before on day trips. The farm was unusual enough to interest a boy who found middle-income habits in a middling large town in the mid-'50s Deep South flat and constricting. What did I have to do except go to school and church, watch Sunday night television—*The Ed Sullivan Show, GE Theater*—and see an occasional cowboy picture? If I had stopped to think, it might have occurred to me that this summer project was only the latest in a series of efforts to "get me *outside*": outside the house, outside my room, outside the cocoon of books and daydreams I had spun for myself. My sisters, extroverted and unbookish, didn't need to be sent to a farm and, if told that they were going to be cut off from friends and fun for a month, would probably have resisted.

These cousins lived on an old farm roughly an hour's drive from us. A big farm, based on several crops and making use of some half-dozen "sharecroppers." I wouldn't have known enough to understand

1

that driving that sixty-mile distance amounted to time travel backward several decades. The farmhouse itself was a hundred years old, a sprawling affair all on one floor, weathered down to the gray clapboard, with tin roof and a veranda that went almost entirely around the outside so as to connect all the rooms, only a few of which had interior doors between them. The whole structure sat on brick pilings a few feet off the ground, and there was no lawn, partly because the huge live oak trees gave too much shade and partly because no one here had time to care much about what the Ladies' Club in town called "beautification." There was a privet hedge, no longer well-tended, that led raggedly up to the veranda steps, otherwise no ornamental plantings.

I stepped up on the veranda behind my parents, and now Aunt Gladys was pushing open one of the screen doors. Out the corner of my eye I caught a glimpse of the two boys, Emmett and Ronnie, loping over from the direction of the barn. Ronnie was two years older; Emmett, a year younger than I. There were also two girls, Louanne and Florence, who, Aunt Gladys told us, were taking a nap, but they would be up directly. On farms like these children are part of the labor force, so Aunt Gladys and Uncle Burton could be said to have a small family—certainly in comparison to the sharecroppers, who usually counted six or eight child mouths to feed, and by the same token extra help with the chores.

The grownups sat down in the faded velvet chairs of the front parlor for the ritual one-hour visit. After an all-around greeting, youngsters were free to go outdoors and get reacquainted. I was always intimidated by my cousins' direct, mischievous stares, their burned-brown skin, and their unboyish, muscled arms. On their side they vacillated between hushed respect for and bald mockery of a citified visitor, but all this was smoothed over by country tolerance for practically anything that comes down the road and by a sense of blood kinship, which in the South annuls many a difference between people.

We walked over to the barn and past it to a fenced-in field where a few pigs, hairy and spotted, were slumped together in the shade. Ronnie picked up a watermelon from a heap benignly stacked next to the fence. "We had a bumper crop of these this year. Can't even give'm away." He heaved aloft the plump, pea-green ellipse, striped with brush-stroked darker green, and flung it to the dozing pigs. A loud *thump*, and then a satisfying spillage of red guts onto the ground: one of the pigs lumbered to its trotters, waddled up to the broken melon, and began troweling and snuffling in it with his snout.

"*Here* pig, sooey, soeey, sooey, *pig*," Ronnie called. None of the other pigs stirred. One of them was a sow, a half-dozen young fastened to her teats like sucking leeches. Her eyes were closed, whether with ecstasy or exhaustion, impossible to tell.

"Let's eat a watermelon," I said.

"If you want to." Ronnie pulled out a pocketknife, flipped it open, bent down, then cut into one of the rinds. He handed me a wedge of dripping melon, red, glazed with silver. It was sweet, but hot. Had I expected it to be cold just because watermelon is always served that way? No one could enjoy this sugary vegetable. I finished what I'd been given, noticing that no one else had taken any. The rest was thrown to the pigs who, this time, contemplated the red and green wreckage but didn't move toward it. For no reason, Ronnie and Emmett let out a war whoop and began running back toward the house. There was nothing to do but chase after them in an improvised game of pursuit.

Now Mama and Daddy were saying their goodbyes, one after the other, down the veranda steps. I wiped my hands on my blue jeans and went to exchange a final hug. "Be good, and do what Aunt Gladys tells you," Mama said as I nodded. They waved goodbye from the blue Packard as it was wheeling around in the drive. Then they were gone. Dust rolled through the air. From the henhouse I could hear clucks and the rusty scrape of the rooster's cry. It had been settled that I was to stay for a month.

"You've got watermelon juice on your chin," Emmett teased me.

"Did you feed him one of those things?" Aunt Gladys asked.

Ronnie told her that I had asked for some. She smiled at me, and I, a little sheepishly at her. "Well, y'all come to supper in ten minutes. I hope you haven't ruined your appetite, Stephen."

After supper we all went into the parlor and sat for a while. My great-aunt Merle, who had lived with her daughter and son-in-law these past ten years, started telling funny stories. The time when Aunt Gladys and Mama, making hand-crank ice cream for a high school party, had got confused and put salt in the custard instead of sugar. The time she'd seen a bum stealing something from out of her car, and she'd just gone over and said if he didn't put it back, she'd tan his hide, and he apologized, and so she gave him a quarter. Aunt Merle laughed at herself and winked at all of us, who laughed appreciatively.

Suddenly the whole room went dark. Uncle Burton said, "Dammit, there goes another one of those fuses," and stamped out of the room. We sat in the dark. Undeterred, Aunt Merle started a story about a fisherman she met last January in Cocoa Beach. (She went to Florida every winter for three months.) After a few minutes, Uncle Burton came back with a kerosene lamp. "Can't find any fuses," he said. "Have to get some more tomorrow." He set the lamp on an end table and then left the room. Not at all disconcerted by kerosene lamplight, Aunt Merle went on describing her curious fisherman. Trembling shadows were cast around the room, especially in the corners. The glass chimney of the lamp reflected in the lenses of her round, gold-rimmed spectacles. She was talking and smiling, but I could no longer hear the words, or rather, I could hear them but not make sense of them. Something about the fishing rod and "… used nightcrawlers for bait."

Gray light. I'm face down on the pillow. I turn and see someone pulling on his pants. "Emmett?" I whisper. Ronnie is already out on the porch; I can see him through the screen door. He begins pumping water into an enameled iron pan. *Shriek-creak-shriek. Splash-wheeze-splash.* I sit up on the edge of the bed. There are my clothes, neatly folded on the rocking-chair arm. The air feels cold against my bare skin. I get up and put on my clothes, make my way to the door. The sun hasn't risen yet. "What time is it?"

"Oh, 'bout five o'clock," Ronnie says, backlit against distant misty trees. "A little after. Want some water?" He holds out a zinc dipper. I take it automatically. The water is icy and tastes metallic, electric. I give the dipper back.

"Where are you going?"

"We got to help Daddy with the south forty." I look at him. "You can go back to sleep, long as you want to. Maybe we can do something this afternoon." From the henhouse, low rasping clucks and the triumphant rooster. I nod dumbly and go back into the bedroom, into the darkness, feeling the rough grain of the floorboards under my feet. To be awake at this hour seems somehow sad and lonely—my last thought before slipping back into bed, into sleep.

A ray of sunlight, like warm glass applied to my face. Clatter from the kitchen, hunger in the pit of my stomach. I scrambled into my clothes again. Out on the veranda and then a few steps to the kitchen. Only Aunt Gladys was there, washing up the last dishes and supervising the next meal, covered pots already steaming on the stove.

She turned and confronted me, her broad, honest face split with a grin. "Hey, boy, you got yourself a good sleep, didn't you? I saved some grits and some eggs and bacon for you." With one swift, unbroken gesture, she wafted a plate from the oven and set it down for me at the long table. Its red-and-white checkered oilcloth covering was scattered with crumbs of biscuit and drops of syrup, plus the occasional fly crawling among them and pausing to feed. Aunt Gladys took a damp cloth and swiped at all this. "Does your Mama let you drink coffee? If I put milk in it? OK, let me pour you some."

I shoveled down my breakfast and took the plate politely to the sink, where it was seized and immediately washed. As she put it into the rack, Aunt Gladys said, "Now you don't have to help me, it's all done, you just go out and play." Only one of us, apparently, realized that the suggestion had a condescending side to it.

Out to play I went, though—at least, if a slow stroll down to the barn, with gaze downturned to watch bare feet scuff up dust can be called play. No pigs in sight this morning. I turned to the barn door and hauled it open to the accompaniment of creaks, feeling the dowel smoothness of the worn wood handle against my palm. Inside, light filtered through cracks between boards and through knotholes, making a second structure of light within the gloom. From a little window up near the angle a long, hard sunbeam slanted downward to the floor, ever widening until it joined a golden trapezoid on the packed dirt. Made of energy only, still it manifested a curious solidity, even with the liquid spin of bright motes caught inside its confines. A pigeon fluttering in and out of the window flew magically through the golden fluid, letting a feather, two feathers, slide most of the way down the light-ramp before they turned aside into darkness.

I closed the door and walked, in my bare feet, over the cool dirt back behind Aunt Gladys's kitchen and then to the outhouse. A crescent moon cut in the door let air filter into a cubicle already heated up by morning sun. The stench and heat were complete and unrelenting, enough to have sent me on my way right then if it hadn't been necessary to stay and adapt to available arrangements. I looked down the hole next to me, my feelings in part illicit, in part terrified. What was down there was what people had inside them and had to get rid of. Years of accumulated human secrets, undeniable yet never publicly acknowledged, lay there below.

Leaning against the wall in front of me was a Sears Roebuck catalogue, its pages fanned open and many of them torn out. I batted through brightly painted illustrations of "bedroom suites," power mowers, hunting outfits, and strands of imitation pearls. Next came the toy section. Most of the wares were familiar to me, and some few of them I already owned. But I was at the age when toys lose their hold over you, without having yet been replaced by much else. I had a bicycle, but neither a motor scooter nor a baseball mitt held much attraction for me. No books were for sale in the catalogue, either. There. It was done. I took one of the order-form pages (softer than the glossy pictures) and used it as intended. A spider deflected from its path went fingering its way up invisible threads and scuttled into a dark upper corner. The door groaned shut behind me. I stood and searched the branches of the fig tree that stood outside for possible fruit, the leathery leaves rustling in the wind, mud below worming its way up between my toes. Some baby figs were there, none of them ripe enough to eat yet.

The only thing I could think of to do was to walk listlessly around to the front of the house and sit on the veranda steps. At a distance I could see the fields and a tractor riding up and down between rows of corn. A white powder was being sprayed into the air—which explained the itchy, sulfur match odor I had begun to smell and which made me double over with a loud *Choo!* My eyes began to water; the sunlight turned liquid, overrunning the cup. Still, I sat. A voice behind me said, "They're dusting the corn today." Aunt Gladys, standing stolidly at the top of the steps, arms akimbo and wearing a straw sun hat set well back on her head.

She began to prompt me with questions, and, with no second thoughts, I answered, telling her as much about our family situation as she wanted to know—or at least as much of it as I understood. It didn't occur to me to be discreet. What adults did and said must be acceptable behavior and so could be told. Unhesitatingly I mentioned the mortgage that had been taken out on the house, readily allowed that my father didn't like his job, and laughed about an occasion when he and my mother had had a squabble about how much time she was spending doing work for the Ladies' Club.

"But they mostly get along real well, don't they? And you're happy as can be to be their little boy, aren't you?" I nodded. "And, look, now, are you having a good time here?" As I stared at her plain, tanned, plump face, it became clear that I was going to have to answer politely rather than truthfully. A month of something close to misery lay ahead of me, but somehow my aunt and uncle must be kept from knowing this. I didn't want to hurt their feelings or seem like a spoiled city brat. Acting skills, already solid from living with my parents, were going to have to get better while I was here.

"Oh, yes, I really like it here. It's a lot different from home."

Aunt Gladys smiled at me, and said, "Good. Well, you just enjoy yourself, we're real glad you came." That was probably acting too. She sighed at nothing in particular and fingered the corner of her mouth, her elbow resting on the top of a hand clasping her waist.

"Aunt Gladys, what do they dust crops for?"

"Kill corn borers."

"What's a corn borer?"

"A worm. It gets into the little ears. It'll ruin a whole field quick as a streak if you don't tend to it." She noticed my watering nose. "Oh, look, honey, you must be allergic to that dust. Whyn't you come inside now and look at a magazine."

I cast about for some excuse but ended up following her into the parlor. She sat me down next to a floor lamp and gave me a copy of *Agricultural Digest*. I turned the pages without much conviction, looking at articles on feed and fertilizer, ads for feed and fertilizer, and, also, crop dust. My eyes didn't stop watering.

Next morning Ronnie asked me if I wanted to go with him and watch them "string tobacco." But what was that? He'd show me when we got to the tobacco barn. Sure, I wanted to go, why not, I didn't have anything special to do. It was a relief to take part in what others were doing, no matter how foreign it sounded. On a big, active farm like this, solitude was noticeable, and the only thing worse than being alone was loneliness observed by the outside world.

The sharecroppers were already there, setting long poles into slots in the wall, next to stacks of green tobacco leaves. Strong twine was fastened to the end of the pole, and then workers began to attach handfuls of leaves to it, the twine braiding in and out among stems until some two dozen clumps of green leaves were secured. The poles, Ronnie explained, would be hung in the curing barn over oil heat until toasted and market-ready. I took all this in. There was a funny sense of circularity in the fact that the workers, with their bony frames, oversized clothes, and nervous blue eyes, were all smokers, puffing away on their unfiltered Chesterfields and Luckies while they worked. Ronnie even persuaded one of them—he called him by his first name, "Floyd"—to give him a cig. Ronnie smoked it expertly and even offered me a drag; but I refused. My parents were categorical about smoking; it "stunted your growth," and I knew there would be trouble if anything got back to them about me and a cigarette. I was a coward, admiring the courage of others without being able to duplicate it.

When Ronnie saw Uncle Burton step down from the red pickup, though, he dropped the cigarette and stamped it out. Then, as a diversionary tactic, he grabbed something from off a tobacco leaf and held it up to my face. A fat green caterpillar—but hairless and with mock blue and black "eyes" marked on its tail, along with a single sharp spine projecting a quarter of an inch from its body, a sort of rhinoceros horn.

"*That's* an ugly thing. What is it?"

"Tobacco worm. It won't bite you." He threw it down. "Sure eats up tobacco, though." He crushed it with his basketball shoe, leaving a green smear on the dirt.

"And cigarettes eat up your lungs with cancer," I said.

"I don't believe that, do you?" Ronnie laughed. "If it was true," he said, gesturing toward the sharecroppers, "sure are a lot of people going to get cancer."

Uncle Burton sauntered up. "You boys having fun?"

I nodded but couldn't think of anything to say. My eyes fell to the ground and the crushed tobacco worm, next to Ronnie's shoeprint, which looked like a drawing of a one-celled animal. "Ronnie found a tobacco worm on the tobacco."

"Yep. That's where they live. Got a lot of'm this year."

"He killed it, though," I said, pointing to the green smear.

"I wish he could kill ever one of'm." Then he turned to his workers and began instructing them. After consultation with a short man wearing a big felt hat, the one named Floyd, he turned to Ronnie and said, "Listen, Floyd's got to get back home and tend to his wife. She's laid up with fever. Why don't you run him home and Steve can go with you for the ride."

By state law you had to be fifteen to have even a learner's permit, but Ronnie already knew how to drive and did so often, license or no. It was still enough of a novelty to seem a treat, so he took the keys from his father with a visible sense of proud investiture. Uncle Burton wouldn't think of letting a sharecropper drive the truck if there was any way not to. Floyd never proposed himself, either, just sat with his arm propped in the window and hummed quietly as we drove down the long dirt road to his house.

It was no better than a shack. A white-painted tire sprouting petunias sat in the front yard, otherwise there was no effort to prettify. The frame house was paintless and leaned slightly. To one side of it sat a battered Oldsmobile, windows open and body rusting, in the spot where, no doubt, it had been deposited years earlier. Five children with white-blond hair, at least one pair of them twins, stopped playing and regarded us gravely as we got out of the truck.

"You all want to come in for a minute?" Floyd asked. We followed him through the open front door. From the second room (there were two) a whining voice called out, "Floy-id, is that you? Who you got with you? Oh, hello boys, excuse me for not getting up, I'm feeling peaked today. Floyd, why don't you get those boys a cookie."

"Where?"

"In the cabinet next to the Frigidaire. There's Fig Newtons."

Floyd rummaged around in the cabinet. "They ain't any Fig Newtons in here."

"Raymond! Eddie! Did you children eat all those Fig Newtons? I *told* you not to eat *any more* of 'm. If I was up, I would whip you good. Floyd, give those children a whack."

Floyd made a despairing gesture. "If you younguns don't start obeying your mother, I'm going to strap you, I'm warning you." The children ran outside without answering; and, there being nothing for us to do inside, we followed them. Floyd thanked us for driving him and saluted as we drove off.

"White trash are all like that," Ronnie said, gunning the engine as he shifted into second.

"They weren't really white trash. She was just sick, that's all."

"They are too. Would *you* live like that? All right then. White trash. They'd starve to death if we didn't give 'm work."

Although each day at the farm was unlike the preceding ones, still they all had a family resemblance. The solitary breakfast, the visit to the outhouse, the inspection of premises by now thoroughly familiar. From time to time there would be some new agricultural process for me to observe at a distance or some chore to take a minor part in. Everyone could see—and I could see that they saw—just how much at a loss I was with the problem of filling my time. My efforts to seem cheerful and busy failed. But no one expected me to duplicate the daily schedule of Ronnie and Emmett, whose chores were considered too strenuous for a city boy. (Or simply too specialized: incompetence couldn't be allowed to slow down the work.)

Then Aunt Merle came up with a plan. "Why don't you pick beans?" I listened. "The field hands are going to be out there tomorrow. They won't mind if you go out, too. Tell you what, I'll give you a quarter for every bushel of beans you pick. It'll be fun and you can make yourself some pocket money."

I wasn't certain how big a bushel was. But obviously it couldn't be *too* hard to fill if, as Aunt Merle said, "You can pick ten of 'm in a morning if you get busy."

From the two dozen bushel baskets stacked inside each other like Dixie Cups at the edge of the bean field, one was withdrawn and turned over to me. It was about half my height and not particularly easy to handle. I joined the "field hands," some half-dozen black women in faded cotton dresses and sun hats, who looked at me and smiled but didn't say anything.

The beans were harder to negotiate than had been suggested. I was instructed not to pluck them by the stem because that would pull the whole bush and break off branches: each bean had to be separated from its stem. Experienced croppers could do this with one hand, the other free to drag the bushel basket along behind. I used two hands, which was adequate but slow. Eventually I learned to use one hand, shearing off the stem with my thumbnail. After a while—gouge, snap, toss—the nail began to pull away from the thumb and a thick, green sludge lodged underneath. I tried other tactics, some temporarily successful. The black women moved farther and farther ahead of me in their rows, singing in unison. The sun flashed and shimmered. Trickles of sweat traveled down my back, and my legs and arms itched. They had been right in saying I would need a hat; the only one available had been too big—it slipped down and covered my eyes. Maybe I should have tried to adjust it. The bushel basket was getting heavier; I felt I was dragging a dead calf behind me. With the effort of resisting this anchor, my heart began to pound. If I could fill just one basket—. My thumb ached and its pulled-back nail burned. The bushes of beans clung fiercely to their

11

pods. The high-low tunes of the hymn-singing got fainter and fainter. My bushel was half full. The sun burned and crackled. My eyes itched and watered. There was the sound of an airplane flying overhead, a dragonfly drone and buzz. Glancing up, I saw for an instant a black-winged shadow, then the magnesium explosion of sun, rays of light stabbing down into my vision. I had to bring my eyes down to the green field—shaking, vengeful green, green as the tobacco worm, a liquid smear of violent green as far as I could see. Everything itched and trembled and burned. White-hot metal being poured, a green earthquake....

Thud. I am sitting on the hot dirt, holding on to my bushel basket, sweat streaming down my face. A woman suddenly comes up. "You all right, honey? Let me help you stand up." I wobble to my feet.

"Excuse me, I gotta go back."

"Yeah, you betta go back and rest awhile." She walks me to the edge of the field, helping me carry the bushel. It is three-quarters full. I keep walking all the way to the house, afraid I will faint. Somehow both the bushel and I reach the shade of the live oaks.

"That's as much as I could pick, Aunt Merle."

A sympathetic nod. "You ought to've had a hat. Here's a quarter for your bushel, baby. Now you go lie down for a while and take a nap."

The bedroom I stumbled into was quiet, hot, empty. I could hear the sound of a tractor growling in the distance, and then the irritable purr of a horsefly, equally loud. The frame house creaked in the heat. I fell asleep.

Dreams, confused, twisting dreams. Voices and faces. Making my way through an underground tunnel, turning sharp corners, moving from torchlight to torchlight, with half-perceived figures ahead of me and approaching from behind. They were about to catch up with me.

The hand on my forehead was Aunt Merle's. "How do you feel?" she asked.

"I feel sick."

"Yep, I think you have fever. I'll get a cold rag." She left and returned in a moment with a damp washcloth, which she smoothed over my forehead. "Take this aspirin."

"I feel like I might have to throw up." An electric current of nausea was coursing up my throat in regular pulses, and the sour aspirin (which I chewed) only added to the queasy sensation I was trying to swallow down.

"Wait just one second, I'll get a pan." But when she brought in a white enamel basin and held it beside the bed, the spasm passed. Still, she stood next to me, holding my head.

"Aunt Merle. I wonder if it was that watermelon."

"What?"

"That watermelon I ate the other day. It might have given me something."

"Maybe so." She looked pityingly at me.

"Aunt Merle? Maybe I better go home."

"You want me to call your Mama and Daddy?"

"I think I better go home if I'm sick."

"OK, baby, I'll call them right now, long distance. Here's this pan, right beside the bed if you get sick." She left the room.

Later, when it was concluded that I would leave the next day, the whole family, one by one, came in to have a look at me. Sick people were a rarity in this house. Everybody felt pity and perhaps a certain awe before someone who had become even more special than he had been.

Ronnie sat at the foot of the bed. "Maybe you picked up a bug over at Floyd's place. Remember his wife was down sick with the fever." I agreed I might have. Ronnie said he was sure I'd get better soon. Floyd's wife was still down with it, but don't worry, I was too ornery for fever to get the best of me. He laughed and punched my thigh, and I tried to take his compliment even though I knew "ornery" hardly described me. Outside, the rooster began warming up for sunset.

Once home, within a few days I was entirely recovered. Our doctor said it was most likely a mild case of sun-poisoning. My mother asked me if I wanted to go back to the country, but I said no, without explaining exactly why. I knew I wouldn't be able to convey the sense of having been superfluous, a useless drag on the smooth-running machine of the farm. Nor did she press the issue.

It was in much the same confiding tone, the following fall, that she asked me if I would like a little baby brother or sister. Because I was going to have one soon. Her soft smile and general air of suppressed excitement made it clear what answer I was to give. In any case, it was hard for me to know what I, the youngest, the "baby" of the family, was actually feeling. But I would have until the following March to prepare myself—and seeing my mother in maternity clothes was part of the preparation. I had heard and read enough to know that she was carrying a small, developing mammal inside her own body, however disturbing that might be to a child's sense of physiological propriety. This growing creature changed her shape; and, what's more, was devouring her very substance, a total dependent that grew larger every day. I noticed that I had come to like going to school more, even though I was afraid of nearly all my classmates. My teacher, Mrs. Virgil, liked me and praised me; and she was not expecting a baby.

Sometime that winter I suddenly became noticeably thin, and more lethargic than usual. Another trip to the doctor, where routine tests for anemia turned up something quite different: "a touch of intestinal parasite." None of us really knew what hookworm was. The doctor explained that infection came through the feet; the simple precaution of wearing shoes outdoors was enough protection from the minuscule larvae, which lived in dirt near livestock. Of course, we all immediately knew where I had picked it up, but nothing was ever said, as though to remark on this obvious fact would somehow be insulting to Aunt Gladys and Uncle Burton.

The cure was simple: little red capsules taken three times a day, and calomel. Within a week I was free of parasites, my hidden, leaching parasites. The word itself, however, lodged itself firmly in my imagination the rest of the school term, a serpentine, negative twin to "paradise," which I'd known for as long as I could remember. By the time my baby brother was born, though, I had put the whole incident out of my mind, or below it, unreflectively caught up in other pursuits. In school, for example, I was learning new words nearly every day— *economy, resolution, represent*—a fund that has gone on building right up to the present. Whether they depend on me or I on them is one of those knotty questions. Now and then a friend asks me (as Aunt Gladys once did) if I'm "having a good time" with them; I always answer yes. On those occasions also, there comes the same rush of eerie emotion that crystallized when my mother, still in her hospital bed, held up a small green-blanketed bundle with a red face peeking out of it and said, "Here. You can hold the baby."

ATLANTA

An explosion of anger not different from any other four-year-old's. Something his Daddy said or did, nothing terrible, but expressing an attitude that a kid can't understand and reacts to by running out the door into the street. No cars or trucks were passing here at the sparsely populated edge of town. A white frame house stood opposite, and a live oak tree's shade tempered summer heat as it billowed up from the asphalt. And then another house, this time brick. He ran up the road, soon aware that he was being followed. "Where you going, boy?"

"I'm going to *Atlanta!*"

They laughed, caught up with him and dragged him back.

He knew nothing about Atlanta except that it was a big town and far away. But the pattern was set: if you don't like your current location, you go somewhere else, at least you try to. A little older, after learning a few things about Georgia's biggest town, after reading *Gone with the Wind*, after hearing about the tall buildings on Peachtree Street and the escalators at Rich's department store (he'd never been on an escalator), he was even more eager. So, when he was twelve, his mother finally went with him on the two-hundred-mile pilgrimage to the beacon city. Her brother had established a goldmine practice up there as a neurosurgeon. The two of them had come from a modest family, but Uncle Andrew's medical practice took him to another level entirely. He'd bought a big white-columned house in exclusive Buckhead, high up among other columned mansions with their enormous lawns. It was clear he fit in well with his country-club neighbors, enough like them to be confident in their company, and yet different, interesting, refreshing.

The old Chevy strained up their serpentine drive, winding around to the back of the house, where it managed to park next to a 1955 cream-and-gold Chrysler. He let his mother take the lead up the back steps into the kitchen where Allie (Alabama) greeted them. She was a nice-looking woman, light-skinned, no longer young, her straightened black hair pulled back into a bun, with high cheekbones and faintly Asian eyes, a feature probably traceable to her Cherokee ancestry. ("They don't come any smarter than Allie," his mother had said.) After a reserved but friendly greeting, she went out into the main part of the house and called upstairs, "Oh, Miz Burns! Miz Burns! Your sister Miz Peggy's here."

As his aunt slowly made her way downstairs, his mother said, "Hey, Lizbeth, how're you, sweetheart?" Aunt Lizbeth grinned and stretched out her arms to welcome a person she called "Darling," before turning to him and saying, "Oh my, look how Little Jack has grown! Give me a kiss, honey!" When she bent forward and presented a cheek, he breathed in an exotic scent, something spicy, something that smelled expensive. At her wrist a chain bracelet dangled, three small spheres that were probably twenty-four carat gold. Another feature he noticed was the streak of white hair above her forehead, so much in contrast with the rest of it, which was dark as shoe-polish.

Aunt Lizbeth had come from a much more leisured background than Mama and Uncle Andrew. Her family owned, and had owned for a long time, several thousand acres of farmland outside town and some upscale real estate in the center. Still, she spoke the same as everybody else and seemed to have identical views about the importance of family and church and being nice to any person you met, no matter who they were, and that most definitely included colored folk. This visit's first conversation took place in front of a family portrait, Aunt Lizbeth and Uncle Andrew dressed up and confidently posed with their boys Andy and Ellis. The youngest cousin hadn't been born at the time of the portrait. This was poor, sweet Tom, who had a birth defect, his condition, if ever spoken of directly, described as "mental retardation."

Jack later heard Allie refer to him as "simple," but she didn't say it in a condescending way.

Aunt Lizbeth touched his shoulder and said, "Jack, why don't you go up and see Tom; he's in his room and I know he'd love to speak with you." She waved him upstairs, ("third bedroom on the left, honey") and drifted into the living room with his Mama. He found Tom lying on his bed, looking at a magazine and humming a tune that did and didn't sound familiar. It was only the second time they'd met, and Jack wondered if he'd be recognized. But Tom called out "Hey, Jack!" and raised his eyebrows to emphasize a crooked smile. They sat and talked, constantly changing subjects, some of them too off-center for Jack to respond to. Tom put a "Jack" into almost every remark he made, which overall gave a feeling of warmth and friendliness. He had a way of plucking at his shirt collar, a shirt that, though clean, was a little frayed at the collar and not ironed. Tom didn't seem to care much what he wore, so nobody else did. He'd been sent to a special school when he was younger. The school told my aunt and uncle that he was the most gifted student they'd ever taught. But that phase had come to an end, and Tom almost never went out now. He would listen to his radio, watch TV, or look at picture books. And occasionally horse around in the back yard. Plus have dinner with his parents and brothers. Mama had told him that Tom had an amazing special skill: if you named a date for any year past or present, he could tell you what day of the week it was. When a lull in the conversation came along, there was a chance to ask him about it, and how he did it. A little pompously he answered, "Yeah, I-I-I can do that, Jack. It's not-not-not hard. I just remember when the d-d-dates are."

"What day ... was ... September 8, 1947?"

Tom looked to one side and whispered something inaudible. He turned back, looked Jack in the eye but seemed not to see him. Then he stuttered, "M-M-onday."

That was surprising and funny, but then who could say if he was right or wrong? Still, when people looked up old calendars and tested him, they saw Tom always got the day right. Jack tried a few more, and got quick responses, but had no way of checking, and then let the game drop. A few days later, when he and his mother went back home, it occurred to him that Tom would have the date engraved in his memory.

No doubt just as memorizable was the day Jack returned eight years later to that big white Buckhead house. He'd spent his first year at Emory out in the Atlanta suburb of Decatur, followed by a summer back home that must have seemed just as long to his parents as it did to him. He got through the three months of vacation by reading and taking aimless drives around town. At some point during the following school year his parents devised a plan to get him off their hands so that he'd be doing something *productive* during the summer holiday. Push the fledgling out of the nest and into the real world, so to speak, and away from all those books. He guessed he'd been the subject of a parental conference. And the result? They found him a job, a job in Atlanta. One of his Mama's girlfriends from high school days had married another of their schoolmates, a man who after college had become an executive at Rich's department store. (That was the one with the escalators). When she asked this old friend if he could find her boy a job at the store for the summer months, he told her he thought he might be able to. With a certain amount of presumption, his Mama then asked Aunt Lizbeth and Uncle Andrew if they would put Jack up for the duration—the house being so large, with so many bedrooms and all.

Luckily, Jack wasn't party to this embarrassing conversation, but the upshot was that he arrived early that summer and settled his clothes and paperbacks in one of the spare bedrooms, the one next to Tom's. Tom was glad to see him, glad he was going to be staying the whole summer, all three months of it. "I just don't know if you'll be happy in that room," he said. "I don't like that room, I wouldn't stay there." Jack looked at him. Maybe there was a little more sadness or nervousness in Tom's face than there used to be. Also, some blackheads that no one had bothered to take care of. Tom's was the melancholy of boredom, no doubt, because he didn't have anything to do. Some people with developmental problems get jobs doing simple work, but apparently the family didn't think that would be suitable for Tom. He just stayed at home.

Later that evening cousins Andy and Ellis breezed in, Andy having had an afternoon of golf, and Ellis out with some of his football team buddies on an excursion whose location and purpose he left vague. Both were good-looking, good-humored boys, Andy one year older, Ellis one year younger than Jack. Andy had well-cut, caramel-colored hair and the smooth, relaxed manners of the new Southern upper class—behavior that only slightly resembled what you expected from the old families back home, sequestered as they were behind the privet hedges and peeling paint of their heritage. Ellis was much darker, with the tight muscles of a quarterback, chest hair sprouting where his polo shirt opened. He liked to make chuckling wisecracks and slap you on the shoulder as he sprang them on you. Perfectly affable boys (family is family), Jack could, even so, tell that they weren't at all interested and that he shouldn't expect to spend much time with them, outside of meals. Which was a relief, though he wouldn't have admitted it to anyone. There was just one token night out when the three of them went to see a war movie (Tom stayed home), but after that Jack was left to take care of his own social life.

At supper, a plate had to be kept warm for Uncle Andrew, who almost always arrived late, given his long hours at the hospital. He swept in just as everyone was getting up from table, greeted Jack with a friendly joke, then sat down to his meal. Jack admired him for being a successful neurosurgeon but was also a little daunted by his unstoppable cheerfulness, rapid movements, loud speaking voice, and rock-solid gaze. Which continued to resonate in Jack's mind as he went upstairs to his room and the stack of books next to a little frilly blue table lamp. He knew he was never going to get on easy terms with his aunt and uncle and the boys. Also, that the fault was as much his as anyone's. He had for a couple of years now been preoccupied with an enormous anxiety, a situation you just can't discuss. And since that subject was off limits, he could hardly talk about anything at all. He was polite and close-mouthed, conventional, unfunny, and unexciting. He knew what he was for them: poor Jack.

The following Monday he set out at eight o'clock for the first day at work. A long bus ride got him to the industrial side of the city, where

21

Rich's warehouse was. The job they'd found for him was anything but a sinecure. He was to help move furniture onto delivery trucks as they pulled up at the loading dock, one after another, several dozen over the eight-hour day. You didn't need any skills to heft outgoing sofas and chests of drawers onto a little tractor-trailer and then offload them into the back of a truck, but it did require muscular strength, and Jack had little. He'd never played sports or anything like that. No matter, the job was what it was. Aching in weird places, he did develop a few new muscles over the following weeks. The other boys doing the same work treated him with a certain deference, doing more of the lifting than he did, so they must have been told he was related to somebody high up in the company. Deference isn't friendliness, though, and he was mostly left alone during lunch break, munching on his ham and cheese sandwich and washing it down with gulps of sweet Coke that burned with carbonation. When he did speak with the other workers, there was always the barrier of education and life habits to get past. The idea that some people were lower down on the social scale than himself seemed a little ridiculous, but on the other hand he was a well-spoken college boy, and the workers were high-school dropouts with pungent country-boy accents. They looked at his copy of *Cousin Bette* with blinking incomprehension (he'd been on a Balzac kick for several months), a puzzlement in no way soothed when he explained it was a French novel. One of the older boys shot him a mischievous grin. Jack guessed the boy thought "French" meant it was pornography. The grin was delivered with a certain amount of respect, so Jack didn't disillusion him.

One evening when the grownups had gone out to dinner at the club, and Tom was upstairs watching TV, Jack went out on the rear screened porch to speak with Allie. Now that the day's chores were over, she'd given herself permission to sit down and smoke a contemplative cigarette. On the low rattan table next to her there was a glass of something with ice in it. "Sit down" she said with unaccustomed enthusiasm. Right away Jack realized she'd been drinking. That was going to make it hard to leave. He remembered a whispered conversation between his aunt and uncle about how Allie would sometimes forget herself and drink too much, which was a shame, but then she was so good when she *didn't* drink, bless her heart. Poor thing, to have that affliction, oh my. On the other hand, Jack hadn't seen her drunk before now, her eyes red, her hand trembling. What was he supposed to say?

He was aware that boys his age didn't hang around with the help. They brought you up when you were little, but then at a certain point you distanced yourself. Well sure, you always spoke to them in a friendly way, but there was no socializing. His decision to come and sit with Allie was based on the fact that she was always nice to him, yes, but also because he'd been impressed by what was happening with colored people in the South. Less than a year ago (and almost exactly one hundred years after the beginning of the Civil War), a Baptist preacher named Martin Luther King had begun organizing peaceful demonstrations in several Georgia and Alabama towns. He wanted to abolish the "separate but equal" policy. When you thought about it, you realized he was right, and Jack decided he should do his part by befriending any colored person he met, to stop being separate. The only such person at present was Allie.

He asked if she had heard about Reverend King. Her dark eyes cut to one side. "Yes, I have. I don't know that much about him." It was a guarded answer. She had her job to think of. But then she straightened up. "They say he preaches the Word very well. That's the main thing. He's a good preacher." Maybe as a way of getting away from dangerous ground, she said, "Listen, Jack there's something you might want to think about."

"That I want to think about?"

"Yes. You know, you're staying here with your aunt and uncle, and they aren't charging you anything, isn't that right?" He nodded. "Well, you might want to do something to show how much you appreciate it."

"Oh. I'm sure—I hadn't thought of that. It's a good idea. Wonder what I should do?"

She drew on her cigarette, paused, and exhaled. "Well, you could maybe mow the lawn."

"Mow the lawn. Yeah, I could do that." He felt embarrassed, almost ashamed. It seemed that he was slower-witted than other people. It took him longer to realize what was actually going on in this or that situation. Unless people said things straight out, he didn't guess what they were feeling. But they never said negative things if they could avoid it, that's not how people were taught to behave. So how were you supposed to know?

Late as it was, the sun hadn't set. So, he went out to the little brown shed where garden tools were stored and found the mower. Allie came with him and showed him how to start it. Not a new machine, it made several explosive noises—*pow-pow-pow*—as it rolled out onto the grass. But it did still run and cut, so he threw himself into the job. The problem was the sloping terrain. You had to drag the heavy thing up and down and around awkward corners of the lawn. In a quarter of an hour his shirt was soaked with sweat and then mosquitoes came. He kept going, even after sunset, because dusk still gave enough light, and it would certainly be cooler now than the next morning. In less than two hours' time the grass was cut. Later on, when Aunt Lizbeth and Uncle Andrew came in, Allie mentioned to them what Jack done. They saw she'd been drinking but didn't want to make anything of it. Aunt Lizbeth turned to him and said, "Oh, that was so nice of you, Jack, thank you, but you know, you really didn't have to do that. We've got a man who mows our lawn. But I'll tell him he doesn't have to come this week! Good night, darlin', thank you so much."

Jack was getting more used to manual labor. Muscles ached less. However, after what must have been planned as a trial period, he was promoted upstairs at the warehouse to a desk job in the Service Department. Five employees there answered the phone and dispatched repairmen to take care of stalled appliances still on their sales warranty. The lesson his mother's executive friend had prepared for him was clear: If you start at the bottom, work hard and don't complain, you will rise to the white-collar level and eventually prosper. There was no need to stress the importance of doing so, it was self-evident, it was the American Way. Again, Jack's coworkers in the office must have been tipped off about him. They were very polite, though politeness quickly wore through to a joking familiarity with one of them, a girl named Lynelle, possibly a year older. Plump, fashion-conscious with her silk blouses, gold circle pin, and frosted blond hair cut like Gina Lollobrigida's, she became his best workplace friend. The second week there, she asked why didn't they go out sometime, see a movie, something like that, if he wanted to. He told her he didn't have a car, but if she had one and was willing to pick him up, they could do it. When he gave the Buckhead address, some pleased guesswork crept into her eyes. All her surmises seemed to have been confirmed when he got in the car that evening. She said, "Oh, I just love your aunt and uncle's house, it's so beautiful!" Also, there was the fact that the grass looked freshly cut.

After the film, something taking place mostly on a beach and starring Debbie Reynolds, she drove him back. It seemed too late to invite her in and, besides, he wasn't sure he was entitled to offer her a drink from the household stock of Scotches and bourbons, which the grown-ups seldom dipped into themselves. Anyway, like all faithful Southern Baptists, Lynelle didn't drink. She suggested they just sit in the car for a while. Soon enough she slipped from under the wheel and moved toward him. On cue, he dutifully leaned over to kiss her. A pleasant, perfumed, close-mouthed kiss, in no way stimulating, sort of like kissing a younger sister. She tried a second, smoochier one, which he accepted. His right hand was on her shoulder, the left hand on her waist—the wrong arrangement if they'd been slow-dancing but it worked here to keep a certain distance. She made one more attempt, and then realized nothing interesting was in the pipeline, so she slipped back under the wheel. "Well, this was just *so much fun*," she said, exaggeration betraying the lie. They said goodnight, see you tomorrow. But at work next morning she was more businesslike and never proposed another date.

The only consistent social life Jack had that summer was with Orville Wyman, a fellow student he'd made friends with earlier in the year. They'd both joined the Drama Club that spring and worked on a play as stage hands for an undergrad production of *Blithe Spirit*, though neither of them had been given an acting part. Orville was a tall string-bean with pale red hair that matched the freckles scattered over his face. A surprising feature was the light in his green eyes. A boy who spoke through his long nose, constantly making sly jokes while one eyebrow cranked itself up a half-inch. Not at all good-looking, and that undeniable fact, added to his awkward, jerky body language and a voice that with no warning would leap up an octave, meant that he'd always be a misfit. So, good company for Jack. He did have a car and was every bit as impressed as Lynelle when he first drove up and parked behind the house in Buckhead. Most often the evening's plan was just to go for beer at a place in Decatur called Manuel's. They'd order a big pitcher, sloshing the brown suds into tall, heavy glasses with vertical creases in them. Sometimes two pitchers would be emptied. The world got fuzzy, it swung wild, it broke out in wisecracks. Orville worked a special vein of humor, a mockery like nothing Jack had ever heard before. Absurd, outrageous, fun-poking, inverted, subversive. In philosophy class that year Jack had read Nietzsche's *Transvaluation of All Values*, and in an odd way it seemed to him that Orville's jokes "transvalued" what everyone thought and believed. Listening to Orville, you felt you could say anything, and anything was *just fine*, so long as it was funny.

And one night he finally said what Jack, without realizing it, had been waiting for him to say. Orville got onto the topic of Hank Dickey, another member of the Drama Club, a blonde boy, athletic and good-looking enough always to be cast as the lead. "Yeah, little old Hank, well, I just wonder now if his last name has had a stimulating effect on his physical development."

Half understanding, but not absolutely sure, Jack asked what he meant.

"I mean his own *thing*, stupid. Did it grow bigger because of his family name?" They both howled to the point of tears, and Jack saw Orville sizing up his reaction. There must have been some sort of reassurance because Orville pushed on with it. "Any time he'll let me conduct an inspection and offer an opinion, I'll be proud to do it! I sure will." Another explosion of giggles. And since the terrain had so far proved safe, he concluded, "Preferably in a motel room."

Jack's open-mouthed stare expanded into a smile. All he could manage was, "Oh my God, Orville." No one had ever said anything remotely like that. In the darkness of the car interior, cutting through beer fuzziness and hilarity he felt everything snap, everything change. A boulder had been rolled away from the cave door.

He took a deep breath. "When you finish your inspection, I volunteer to offer a second opinion." Orville hooted a drawn-out "Ah-ha-ha-ha!" Not because what Jack had said was so very funny but because he was relieved. The truth, which Orville had guessed at, was out. They both were in the same category. They could talk.

"Out." That was the word. Orv said he'd been "out" for several years now and explained what that meant. It didn't mean he told everybody about himself. It meant he'd "come out," made his social debut on the "gay scene," and now had sex with men. Jack had never heard the term "gay" or even "camp," and certainly not "out." Over the next weeks, Orv became his instructor, feeding him the terms, the concepts, and even a description of the specific acts that went with being gay, not all of them sounding especially appetizing. It occurred to Jack that Orv wanted them to try out at least a couple of those together. He didn't, though, feel any attraction to his buddy, no more than to Lynelle. Orv fairly soon got the message, and there was the impression that being turned down was commonplace for him, nothing to get upset about. Then he made a pronouncement: Jack and he were "sisters," that is, friends who didn't sleep together. Jack, from his subordinate standpoint, didn't have enough authority to object to the idea that he and Orville were in some sense "girls." Nor did he like the way Orv referred to some of his gay friends (almost always with a note of contempt) as "she" or put a mocking "Madam" before their names. Or if they had pretensions, he called them "queens." Sure, you could see the humorous logic of it: if you loved Adam, you must be Eve. Yes, but Jack didn't think that men were ever women, not really, just because they liked other men.

Orv took him to a gay party, a gathering of about twenty men in a large, expensively furnished apartment belonging to one of his friends. There was a falling-off of noise when they strolled in together, but, soon enough, the chatter and hoots of laughter resumed. Several people drifted over and asked questions, sizing Jack up. He enjoyed the attention as much as he felt embarrassed by it. He got the feeling that

Orv was showing him off like a trophy. A "virgin" to boot. Jack was a little surprised at some of the insults Orv's friends aimed at him, but Orv didn't seem to mind, just laughed and improvised a few insults in return. But nobody insulted Jack. He was the new kid on the block, interesting for that reason, if no other.

As people began leaving, the host, whose name was Connor, asked Jack if he wanted to stay the night. Jack looked at him. Not particularly attractive, but not ugly either. He shyly nodded. He didn't want to be a virgin any more. It was time for him to "come out."

After everyone had gone, Connor ushered him into the bedroom. At an angle to the window was a canopy bed, something Jack had never seen outside the movies. On a mahogany nightstand next to it, a pewter tankard held a single yellow daffodil. Jack wondered if everything had been staged in advance. He and Connor stripped to their briefs and climbed in under the canopy. Fumbling embraces, kisses, tongues. It felt strange holding another person's body, this one plumper and softer than his, with very smooth, hairless skin. Connor soon realized Jack didn't know the first thing, in fact, was petrified. They were both doing the best they could, but—with no results. After a while, Connor said, "Well, good night, young fella. I think that's enough for now. Let's get some sleep."

Naturally Jack couldn't. The bed seemed too small. He was disappointed. Not so much in Connor as in himself. Mostly himself. Hopelessly shy, inexperienced, too sincere to be anything but clumsy. He knew he wanted *something*, but what exactly? Not this. Unable to be more precise, he fell back on the all-purpose romantic idea of "love." His host, the canopy, the daffodil, none of that fit. He'd have to wait until the real thing came along.

There were no more gay parties that summer, and Orville seemed a little disappointed that Jack hadn't got much out of the first one. Orv wanted the best for his protégé, wanted him to thrive and flourish. But at least Jack now had the freedom to talk about being (that mysterious new word) *gay* with him, learning at second-hand what it was going to mean for his future. Occasionally, another gay friend would join them for a pitcher of beer at Manuel's, but Jack never saw any of them independently. One time, when Orville came by to pick him up (they'd planned to see a movie), Jack invited him in to meet Aunt Lizbeth. But he was so awkward and fake-humorous, it was obvious she didn't know what to make of him. And by extension, what to make of her visiting nephew. She gave Jack a funny look when he and Orville left together. It was the only time Orv entered her house.

Besides, she was busy with social plans. Because Andy and Ellis were part of the country-club set and because girlfriends of theirs had been making their social debut that season, she felt she should host some sort of party. Her dilemma was that evening parties all involved drinking. She was a Methodist and therefore shouldn't have anything to do with alcohol, especially if young people were involved. True, she occasionally did have maybe *one* Old-Fashioned, but that didn't mean she would host a party where drinks were available to people in their teens and who would be driving. The solution: to host an early breakfast after one of the dances. These breakfasts were a staple of the coming-out ritual, giving the youngsters time to decompress (and sober up) from the dances before going home to sleep. The standard hour for a post-dance breakfast was five o'clock and typically it lasted two hours. There was a brief argument between her and the boys, who wanted to serve some punch, even though it was just breakfast. But she put her foot down: no drinking.

The week, and then the eve of the party arrived. At dinner Aunt Lizbeth said, "I know you are a good sleeper, so I hope people won't wake you up when they get here early tomorrow morning." He shook his head, smiled, and said he doubted they would. "Because you have to get up and go to work tomorrow, and you *will need* your sleep." She looked at him rather intently.

To fill the silence, he said, "That's right, I do have to go to work, same as ever." But then: "Oh wait, actually, today's Friday. Not working tomorrow." She stared and murmured something indistinct, as though she didn't quite see the point. It came to him then that she was embarrassed, well, almost guilty, because she hadn't invited him to the breakfast. Why? It hadn't occurred to him that he *should* be invited. He didn't know any of his cousins' friends, wouldn't have been able to talk to them comfortably, hadn't attended any of the dances, and, besides, didn't have a tux or dinner jacket. Oh sure, you can always rent one but, look, Jack was just staying there, a guest, family, not really part of their social life. So that was that.

Uncle Andrew hadn't come in from work yet, no doubt because some operation was turning out to take longer than anticipated. He always had the discipline to do things right and had sometimes been known to operate for fourteen hours straight. When Jack went upstairs, he saw Andy and Ellis had already gone out for their evening, though he noticed a faint scent of bay rum lingering in the air. Meanwhile, there was Tom, standing at the door of his room, leaning against the frame, but also more or less constantly in motion. He said, "They're getting ready for the party, aren't they." The bustle and clatter downstairs had begun to make him feel nervous. Tables had been brought out on the big terrace behind the house, and the caterer was now putting linen cloths on them, to be followed by an array of carefully arranged glasses and cutlery. Allie, working overtime, would help the caterer produce huge platters of scrambled eggs, bacon, and toast for the guests. Plus, big pitchers of orange juice.

Tom and Jack talked for a while then went to bed. Sleep did finally come; but then he woke startled when guests began arriving shortly before five. He got up and padded over thick carpeting to the window, his hand parting the silk curtains slightly. Outdoor spots threw bright light onto the tables and chairs. A pretty girl wearing white organza drifted like a lotus out onto the terrace, followed by her escort, perfectly comfortable in the tux he owned. Conversation and laughter. Jack had to be careful not to open the curtains much, so that no one would notice him. More couples, all good-looking, all well-dressed. The largest table had an elaborate centerpiece of flowers mixed in with gilded cattails. Juice and coffee were poured, but no wine or bourbon. Still, Jack saw one of the boys off to one side (clearly not a Methodist) sneak a flat metal flask out of this hip pocket and take a swig from it. Eventually, Aunt Lizbeth came out and gestured everyone to their seats, including Andy and Ellis. The platters of eggs and bacon followed. Noise levels rose.

Jack slipped back under the covers and lay awake for a while. In a few days it was going to be his birthday. Soon it would be time to go back to classes and a dorm room. Two more years of being an undergraduate. And by now he was sure he'd be going to graduate school, the only question being, where. He thought, I'll apply to Columbia. I'll go to New York. There are more of us there, that's for sure. I'll find the right person. It was a comforting thought, even though based on zero knowledge. He fell asleep.

Waking again a couple of hours later in morning light, he looked out through the curtains at the wreckage left by the party, then slipped back into bed and read another chapter of Balzac, which left only two more before the end. When it was time for breakfast—*his* breakfast— he closed the book and got dressed. At the top of the stairs, something made him think of Rich's escalators, how they went not only up, but down. So maybe *those* should be called de-escalators. Walking downstairs was also de-escalating, though not as smoothly. Tom was there in the breakfast room, wearing one of his frayed shirts, this one a brown plaid. His milky cereal seemed to require total concentration. Jack caught a glimpse of Allie, still at work in the kitchen. Tom's head lifted as he looked up with a pleased smile. "G-G-Good morning, J-J-Jack. Guess what. I just wanted to t-t-tell you, in case you didn't know the answer. One hundred years ago t-t-today was a Monday. It wasn't a Saturday. That's right, it was a M-M-Monday. A hundred years ago, you would have to go to work. But you don't have to today."

BLUE ROSES

When Edgar said, "Yes, us too," I was surprised that he and Miriam were calling it quits; but even more by his "too," which linked their separation to Renée's and mine. I was sitting down, elbow resting on my worktable, the phone crackling in my ear. A patch of sunlight made one part of the carpet a brighter red than the rest, and the room's atmosphere became more resolute, more final, as though a bottle cap had just been tightened.

"Sure, I'll be glad to help you move." That's what I said, but with a flicker of inward resistance at the thought of all the packed-up possessions that would have to come down a flight from Edgar's apartment on Thompson Street. He explained that he was shipping out in two stages, though, and that someone else had been conscripted to deal with the really big things. "Well, I'm glad you realize you're dealing with a 98-pound weakling who can barely lift a beer mug, let alone your KLM speakers." That was meant to defuse the over-earnest tone of the conversation. It almost did. I asked who his other helper was but didn't recognize the name. Edgar and Miriam bought in and then cashed out on so many relationships their friends often didn't know each other.

After we said goodbye, I sat down and thought about them while doing mechanical tasks like sharpening a pencil and putting scattered papers in one or another drawer. I'd known them for a long time, but we really didn't see each other that much after we all moved to New York. It turned into one of those serviceable linkages between couples who check in with each other from time to time, never growing closer, but never allowing the friendship to peter out altogether. Once or twice a year, they would have us to dinner or we them, and the reunited foursome always managed to discover a recent trip or project to talk about, a new book or movie—anyway, enough to underpin four courses and the strong coffee served afterward. Those meals, which Renée and I put together with the help of Julia Child, required a three-day lead time for successful preparation, a labor-intensive enterprise we weren't willing to wade into for anyone but Edgar and Miriam. I remember one of those evenings we were cooking up a batch of *crêpes flambées* for dessert, which involved heating the little sweet crepes in a sauce of unsalted butter and Grand Marnier. Watching us fumble through the process, Edgar decided the burner under the saucepan probably needed adjusting. He bent to look and somehow his tie fell forward into the gas flame, caught fire, and had to be swatted with a dish towel that Renée handily flapped against his chest. We all laughed, and in the key of hilarity Edgar took his dessert still wearing that blackened silk stump.

They were New Yorkers originally, but I met them while they lived in Atlanta. Edgar taught English at the university, and Miriam (like me) was in her last year of undergraduate studies in French. Faculty status invested him with authority, and his willingness to accept me as a peer only partly cancelled the distinction in rank. They were, as I said then, *formidable*. Miriam seemed a chalk or two above the rest of the students because of her professor husband, her splashy designer dresses, her blue eyelids, her hair set low on her forehead like a maharanee, long black hair that she often let hang down her back. She had a deep, surrendered smile that exposed her gums, a slow combustion of generosity that her friends would always move closer to, hoping to absorb the glow. Edgar, on the other hand, made a point of never smiling, though you could see him struggling against the temptation. I always remember him in fast-forward motion, nervous, jagged, his professorial verbal style a sort of counterweight to Miriam's softness. He was tweedy, critical, manic. He cultivated a brushy, unkempt thatch of pale red hair, smoked a pipe, and had a way of characterizing women as "magnificent"—well, when he didn't call them the four-letter opposite. Some of his macho bluster

I connected to an enthusiasm for Norman Mailer, who was his favorite contemporary writer. He and Mailer were Brooklynites, which they'd both experienced as a thing to overcome. But it always struck me as an example of protesting too much. It's not so easy to appropriate the old Hemingway swagger.

Anyhow, it was instructive fun for a twenty-year-old Southerner, still more or less a clueless undergraduate, to see Miriam and Edgar. They served martinis, and, as an appetizer, maybe artichoke leaves and drawn butter, or *foie gras* and flatbread. Dinner might be sauerbraten, which I'd never had before, and dessert, say, a *bavaroise à l'orange*, also unknown to me. Afterward, there would be espresso served in little black basalt-ware demitasses (an item in the Museum of Modern Art's Design collection, I later learned). Miriam used a handsome stainless-steel Italian coffeemaker consisting of two separate parts that screwed together. When the connection was tight, you put it over a gas flame, and a few minutes later the aromatic black liquid would shoot up from beneath into the container at the top. Miriam would drop a shaving of lemon peel into each demitasse, a refinement they picked up during trips to Rome. All of this fascinated me, and I tried, with only partial success, to duplicate their connoisseurship, their intake of wine and high-octane gin, their mocking condescension toward anything middle-class, all the traits that set them apart from other people I knew. Though the university offered a degree in Romance language, it was a long way from the Latin Quarter, and we all knew that Miriam and Edgar would flee Atlanta and go back to the Northeast the instant it became possible. Edgar got a job at NYU the year after I met them. Not totally by coincidence, I began graduate school at Columbia at the same moment, cheered by the thought that I was going to live in the town that had produced them and, in theory, other people just as smart.

After Renée and I began living together, I brought her to meet them. It wasn't an instant success. I suppose Miriam and Edgar were a little jealous, and to Renée they must have seemed like in-laws. During the introduction, a gleam came into Edgar's eyes, but I don't think she noticed it. Because Renée was small, honey-blond, and finely made, with a dancer's springy step and the Comp Lit graduate student's witty take on everything, she made an impression wherever she went. But I was sure Edgar would never poach because, after all, we were friends. Meanwhile, it didn't take me long to see that Renée was nice to Miriam and Edgar mainly for my sake; to her they just weren't quite.... I don't know what descriptive term she would have used. But we all bumped along with no visible strain and soon settled into a less intense format of cool, friendly sociability constructed around meals, concerts, and plays. What became more apparent in time was the vulnerability that Edgar's bluster and Miriam's competent stylishness no longer fully concealed. By appearing to have high artistic standards and no illusions, they were simply substantiating their worthiness to be *your* friends. They didn't in fact demand impressive opinions or brilliant conversational performance from Renée and me, or not as much as you'd think. Despite all that social life, all that travel and name-dropping, they were a little lonely. In fact, sometimes I got the queasy feeling that we were their closest friends.

One more oddity: Edgar had begun popping out with compliments on a supposed hipness he saw in us. Renée had a history (almost a rap sheet) of leftwing activism, and once we were together, I followed her lead. Our countercultural credentials included a hodgepodge of part-time work, cannabis, unemployment, writing, scene-making, a half-chosen, half-unavoidable bohemianism. We had friends that would probably have been too extreme even for Edgar and Miriam along the sliding scale of unconventionality. Sure, we liked our far-out friends, the coffeehouse Che Guevaras, the drugged-out gurus, the flamboyant cross-dressers, but we (or at least I) also liked or at least admired Miriam and Edgar. Probably every couple feels as though the middle path is the one they've chosen, if it is really a choice.

When Renée and I decided to separate, Edgar and Miriam were impressed, they said, at how well we had handled things. We'd explained to them that we still planned to be friends, and they took us at our word. Friends: in fact, it wasn't as easy as that. Though we could no longer hack living comfortably under the same roof, we hadn't managed to snap our fingers and just feel nothing about each other. There was this awkward, searing attachment that flared into curse-words whenever we happened to meet. More than a year passed before it was possible to get through a conversation calmly. Miriam and Edgar were told of our *intention* to part amicably, but not how it worked out in practice, to judge by the broken plates one of us had to sweep up off the floor. I could see, too, that they were partly scandalized at how easy it was for us, thinking maybe we hadn't really loved each other. But they never stated that qualm directly.

I wondered if it was something like superstition that led Edgar to ask for my help when he moved, thinking my talismanic presence was going to make his own Independence Day turn into a celebration. When I got to his place (Miriam wasn't there), I asked a few oblique questions. He said that they meant to separate as husband and wife but continue as friends, the way Renée and I had done. "Miriam is still angry," he admitted with a half-smile. Which had to mean that the decision to split up was Edgar's. I nodded and signaled silent empathy. The obligatory cardboard boxes, waiting for us to heft them, made an irregular ziggurat in the middle of the living room, a clear challenge to my tendency to shrink from manual labor. Anyhow, after half a dozen trips up and down the stairs together, Edgar asked me simply to wait by his green Peugeot, to be a watchdog for thieves or meter maids, while he brought down the rest of his stuff. Because New Yorkers almost never drive in the city itself, I hadn't seen that car for a long time. Edgar brought it back from France the year he taught in a university over there, about a hundred and fifty miles south of Paris. I'd been in the Peugeot only twice before. The first time was two springs ago when Renée and I went for a weekend at Edgar and Miriam's house in the Berkshires. An involuntary memory, which kept me occupied waiting out there on the street, in the cool weather of late October.

The house was a gingerbread white elephant, a legacy Edgar had inherited from two maiden great-aunts who had lived there year-round for several decades. One of them was artistic and had painted the walls inside with simple murals of dignified, faceless ladies in long dresses, watering flowers with the help of spouted cans (those, too, painted with flowers). The gracefully feminine figures were no doubt some idealized version of the aunts themselves. Edgar had poetically left their murals untouched. The garden ladies were a fresco for the kitchen, but there were other floral decorations elsewhere in the house. Thinking back, I remembered that the bedroom they gave us had wallpaper not only on the walls but also on the ceiling—in an improbable pattern of blue roses. The paper was in such bad condition from decades of dampness Edgar had painted over most of it with a thick coat of white. But wherever a blue rose was intact, he had left a round opening in the paint, so that, lying on the bed, you still had the benefit of a dozen or so nostalgic peepholes into the Massachusetts of 1918.

It was chilly that spring, but by noon we were able to sun a little. For seating, Edgar had set up folding chairs on the lawn in front of the house, not far from a hammock, a watering can, a lilac that was on the verge of blooming. Everything as pleasant as can be except for a black-fly swarm that kept dive-bombing us. Eventually Miriam brought out a few lengths of mosquito netting and broke into a giggle as she draped them over our heads. We laughed, too, but didn't take the netting off. Still, one or two flies managed to get through (there were tears in the fabric) and annoy us. We must have made a funny tableau out on the lawn, shrouded in our black, defensive veils, mourning some unspecified deceased relative or friend. Strains of Mozart's "Hunting Quartet" flooded from the stereo indoors out into the yard where we were—violin echoing violin, cello underscoring viola. Edgar was an ardent music maven, and, though I seldom heard music in a hall, hundreds of classical recordings lined the walls of my apartment; so, we used to talk about music endlessly. He reminded us that the "Hunting Quartet" had been used in the film *The Rules of the Game*, which I'd seen a couple of times, without remembering the soundtrack or much of the plot. Adultery in country-houses? Something like that.

After supper that night Renée and I talked in our bedroom, glad to have the friendly supervision of the roses overhead. We undressed and jumped under our crinkly quilt, shivering from the chill, and held each other until the bedclothes got to a bearable temperature. She told me she really wished she could get Edgar to stop patting her on the bottom. I spluttered a protest. "What the—?" But there was no chance she'd ever make a big issue of it. Edgar had headed off objections one evening a couple months earlier by telling us a story about pinching some ridiculous faculty wife and then having her pompous husband call up after the party and yell at him (in his absurd German accent) to "keep his hants off my vife!" Renée and I had laughed cooperatively at this figure of fun without realizing we were sealing *her* fate. Shortly after Edgar's bottom-patting began, she learned to be wary of him when he'd had more than three martinis—which was practically any time he was a guest or a host. Renée was feminist and that meant I was supposed to leave the problem to her. Besides, she didn't want to give him any excuse for lumping me together with the German professoriate. I wasn't sure how I felt about this, but if your wife is a feminist and says she can handle something, you'd best let her do it. She sighed and chuckled. A very small draft of cold air moved through the bedroom from some unknown source, a loose window probably. But, with our arms wrapped around each other, we managed to ignore it and fall asleep.

The second visit to the country (and the second ride in the Peugeot) was the October just after Renée and I had separated. I came by myself. Black flies had long gone, and the blazing autumn trees were so clear and sharp they looked like bouquets of bright flowers under a bell jar— orange maples, yellow chestnuts, red pin-oaks all clumped together. In the orchards, crooked old apple trees quietly surveyed a scattering of bruised windfalls. I helped Miriam gather cattails, dried ferns, and other tastefully handsome weeds to take back to the city, where sheaves of them would be put in earthenware vases next to the fireplace.

At night we sat by the brick fireplace, heating up big snifters of brandy, then taking perfumed sips that carried the fire down our throats. We talked about the "old days," Atlanta, the marvelous and ridiculous times we'd had together over the years. And how you couldn't really get good

39

watercress or fresh mushrooms in America, not the same as in France. We didn't talk about Renée; and there weren't any available bottoms for Edgar to demonstrate admiration for. Yet he did land a couple of light claps on my shoulder before I went upstairs at bedtime. (I know: very strange.) Next morning, bird calls woke me up, and I saw the roses floating overhead, through the holes in their surrounding white paint. I lay and stared mindlessly at them until time for breakfast. I had a premonition that I wouldn't be coming back to that house again. What didn't occur to me was that it was going to be the last time I saw Miriam and Edgar together.

Seeing the half-loaded Peugeot outside his apartment building the morning of the move reminded me that in fact I *hadn't* been back. I wondered, too, what Edgar planned to do with the house. Close it up, sell it, maybe? He had brought down all his belongings now. Most of them I recognized, one or two from the country place. There was a handsome collage done by Miriam's father, who taught painting at NYU. There was a bottle of Beefeater gin; some blue enamel kitchenware; several nicely framed Hogarth prints from the *Marriage à la Mode* series, sooty ink on fine cream paper; a box filled with shoes and shoe-trees; and some framed *belle époque* posters from France.

It's standard opinion that material goods are trivial, but at this moment, with Edgar and me, in a kind of male reticence, not saying anything, these objects, these items from Edgar's personal history museum, seemed weighty as much in psychological terms as their actual poundage. No doubt it would have been more dignified for him simply to have said goodbye to Miriam and consigned all the things they jointly owned to the past. Yet I didn't blame him for wanting a few familiar reference points in his new bachelor pad. They would bring a note of continuity and comfort, which he'd clearly need. But those shoe-trees were sort of nakedly mournful. That wasn't something that could be said because Edgar and I were pretending there was nothing unusual in the move. We were sophisticated, hip, unflappable. Right.

I noticed a truck identified as *Broadway Maintenance* parked in front of a tall streetlamp nearby. A cherry-picker at the end of a telescoped crane was lifting a man up to the top of the lamp pole so that he could install a new bulb. Obviously, they have to be replaced at times, but I'd never seen anyone do it. A few expert movements and then down came the cherry-picker, the workman holding on to a burnt-out glass pumpkin, which looked surprisingly large next to his chest. I wondered how long bulbs lasted on average and whether the same man in the same truck would be back a year from then to remove the one he was about to install.

At Edgar's new address, our task cranked into reverse. The difference here was that an elevator had to be negotiated. Its door wanted to close on us before we'd emptied each load. Infuriating how much trouble moving is (and I should know, having done it so often). As I dragged some things along the hallway, a door opened and a woman's head popped out to see who was making all the noise, a paranoid little Yorkie at her feet meanwhile barking at me, all to no avail. I pushed on to Edgar's apartment.

Its floor was bare except for accumulating piles of boxes and suitcases. Skewed quadrangles of light from the southern windows sprawled across the parquet. I didn't go down for the next load and said I wanted to have a look at Edgar's new surroundings. There was more to it: I was remembering a similar apartment I once lived in, with the same kind of southern light. I'd taken it for several months during a period when Renée and I had done a trial separation, less than a year after we first moved in together. We eventually patched things up; and said the relationship, since it had survived such a serious test, was now stronger than it had been. We were in denial about that. When couples start to discuss their "relationship," like it's some third party they're living with, things are already on the way down. My apartment hadn't been as clean as this one, but what can you expect on the Lower East Side? I liked living there, though, in the thick of the East Village's twenty-four-seven carnival, the street politics, the lifestyle, the rainbow colors. Was it around then that Edgar began listening to the Beatles and letting his hair grow longer? I think so.

He brought in the last few things, and we talked, a little artificially, about the parquet floor and the fixtures. I congratulated him on the southern exposure, the view downtown. The topic of Miriam didn't come up. He gave me his office number at school, which I'd never used, saying it would be a while before the telephone company got around to his order.

It wasn't easy to absorb the anemic smile he mustered as our eyes met and parted. The sworn pact of breeziness faltered. I'd always thought of Edgar as well defended, but chinks in the armor were showing. Every word dangled like a sword on a thread ready to tear through the nonchalance we always used with each other. My goodbye handshake tried to convey solidarity, reassurance, warmth, joined to the right kind of detached awkwardness. The rituals of male bonding, I guess, and I have to say I hated it. Finally, Edgar told me not to forget to call Miriam. I promised I would.

I saw them, separately, in the months that followed. Not often enough, admittedly. A funny unease surfaced when I tried to be social with them as one divorced single to another. Conversations kept losing momentum and lapsing into parched silence. I know they remained on speaking terms, but Miriam began seeing a therapist, and Edgar spent a week in the hospital because an ulcer had gnawed a dime-sized hole in his stomach. He didn't end up liking single life as much as he thought he would—no surprise to me. When the novelty wears off, what exactly is the point of waking up next to a different face several times a month, not nearly as entrancing as it had seemed the previous night?

I'd be surprised if Miriam ever smiled her gum-exposing smile at Edgar again. I keep wondering whether I ought to consider myself (and Renée) as responsible, in some sense, for what happened to them. Our supposedly "amicable separation" might have been a catalyst. I felt some guilt, whether justified or not. Anyway, I will never know the truth of it because the rules of the game between Edgar and me banned (as just too uncool) any earnest efforts at self-revelation. That restriction remained in force, and of course we no longer had Miriam to smooth over the disconnect. Longer and longer intervals came between each meeting. In time, we stopped seeing each other. Also, I noticed that Miriam never called; so, eventually, I stopped calling her.

Another question that keeps coming up, no doubt because it's beside the point, is whether the bedroom ceiling of their guest room in the country has been entirely whitewashed now, with no roses currently visible. If it has, memory could still see them. Not to mention other images that appear when little tears in the fabric of consciousness let things slip through, uncomfortable nonsense that we've tried to screen out. But Edgar may have left the house as it was. If the roses are still there, then so are the ladies, watering cans in tow, incorrigible in their determination, despite the ravages of weather, to plant something hardy, to get it to grow and splash some color on their kitchen walls.

KICK

He remembers some, not all of it. Footsteps in the hall outside his door. New York is for loners. He looks at the long hands of the clock behind its glass cover, but he's not thinking about what's happening right now, no, just remembering. This spring is like the last one, the same steps outside, the same temperatures. In a month it will be hot again, and he'll use air-conditioning, just like then.

The second hand of the clock moves because the current makes it move. Midnight on a clock looks the same as noon. Blue-sparking electricity. Trees glimpsed through the window do the same things this year as last, breaking out in shiny buds, not minding if soot comes down on them. If he's going to get off his rear end and do something, he's going to have to soon.

Last spring he took Granisin, picked up a medium-sized plastic tube filled with cherry-red tablets. Prescribed for him by the Chinese—maybe Japanese—Doctor Hsi, which is it? Anyway, not Vietnamese. But Carmencita didn't seem to have any bug, so where did he get it? You know what, he catches everything. Fuckheads in the platoon used to laugh at his skin rashes; "jungle rot," they called it, pointing at him in the showers. Chuckles and steam, butt-naked guys right out of boot camp horsing around with no idea what was in store for them. But you had to laugh. Not so funny, though, when you were clawing at it under your fatigues like an idiot, staring at your nails, getting hung up on the little harvest of dirt, skin, and blood under them. He had to cut them to the quick so he wouldn't scratch holes in his skin.

Footsteps again.

Last spring was Carmencita's. She had this way of striking poses, skinny, arms akimbo, right hip jutting out to one side, "Oh stop reading that damned book," she'd say, "and pay attention to *me*." His piss ran red with the dye in the Granisin, and she laughed at it; people had always laughed at him, never could figure out why. Not tough enough, too much of a candy-ass. Didn't matter if it was medical, she still laughed. "I don't have anything," she said, "so where'd you get clap, you sick fuck?" He raised his hand at her and she made a face, kept ragging him till he slapped her, and she slapped him back, and he slapped her back, which they both sort of thought was funny. But hookers should keep their clothes on until night, when you turn the lights off, to keep you guessing.

He thinks he can decide soon. All the equipment is there, nothing's missing, so if he decides not to kick, he can get back on without wasting any time. It's been a while and he could use a hit, get fixed, it would feel good. Which it doesn't now, hairs standing up on the back of his neck, the icy sweat, nausea in his knotted gut, salt burn in his eyes. The blond hairs on his forearms stand up too, like in wintertime, or when there's too much air-conditioning. So, like, he needed to, soon, one way or the other.

There are different flavors to pain, different ways to hurt. Bone pains were the most fucked-up, he decided. He lay in the Japanese hospital, meditating by the hour on the long note of pain in his thighbone, like a car horn that wouldn't turn off. They never gave him enough morphine to kill all the sensation, just enough to bring it down to manageable levels, or what *they* figured was manageable. "Best medical practice," haha. During his hitch he had three different wounds and gathered a lot of data on the pain subject. Fifty-seven varieties of pain, and jungle rot was nothing in comparison. With that came a bonus expertise in medicines, though Granisin was a new one. He's seen pain from several angles, and which is more interesting? Carmencita said giving was better than receiving. She pinched, slapped, and bit a little, nothing else. Plus, the tongue-lashings, but that was only to provoke him. Still, for her, pain had to be personal. When she got a burn from the iron, she didn't like it. She cussed and complained, *that* wasn't what she wanted. Just when *he* gave it, and then she would cling and cling, her nails digging into his skin so that he did end up receiving, just not so much. She whispered, "Baby, what I do to deserve the way you treat me?" but he wasn't really expected to answer.

Click of high heels on the tiled floors outside. Someone always coming or going. Carmencita had no patience with his infection; he wasn't supposed to be weak. When he said he'd been to a doctor, she turned red and screamed at him. "I'm really, *really* angry this time!" And she sneered at the red piss and provoked him. The heaviest period of the whole time they were together. Remember the way it swung when she bent over him, making a face: a big gold cross with a purple stone. Must have copped it from somebody, it looked like it cost a lot.

Carmencita didn't really like pain as such. She was never able to fix without saying "Ouuuch...." He started doing it for her and then things went OK, she never minded again, it was part of the picture. She brought the works to him, the old brown belt, held them out, with a kind of grinning leer, her head cranked to the left, her lashes black against her cheek. The bleached whiteness of her teeth, slightly protruding like a rabbit's. And after they fixed, she would sit and stare at the spike for a long time as the rush came on. He picked up that quirk from her, though he didn't know what it meant. You meet people, you exchange habits. The buds broke open and turned dark green, he called her his fallen angel. Footsteps. People were there, then they went away, and you never saw them again.

He was one of the few in his platoon who'd managed to keep a watch. And he had this habit, on nights he was pulling guard, of looking at it every fifteen minutes or so. You could duck down and hide the pencil flashlight under your helmet so nobody could see the light. Focus it on the green needles of the watch, which didn't ever have to be wound. He paid a lot for it, bought it from a noncom he met in a bar in Saigon. That was his last three-day pass, and the money could have bought plenty, but he didn't mind. The watch is gone now, lost it when he was hit the third time. Hard to keep things. They show up, they vanish. Hard to give up junk when you've lost everything else. Hard to win a war when you're losing it a little more every day. Anybody who had two brain cells realized they weren't going to win it after the Tet Offensive. Outnumbered, outmaneuvered, out of luck.

But he keeps on remembering last spring. The stretch between now and then is too fuzzy, not much comes back. Because nothing happened, nothing but smack, and the whiteness, the way it turned his skin to vinyl, to hard white plastic. It looked dead and white and felt like piano keys under your fingers. But last spring is cherry-red, the buds on the trees were greener, more alive. Back then he told people he wanted to get into film, write a screenplay for a picture about what it was really like over there. He remembers telling Paul that because he told Paul everything. They were sitting in the garden of the Museum of Modern Art; they'd just seen a movie and were having a cup of coffee. Cool moment. Paul had let his silky black hair grow like a freak's and it looked good, if you like freaky. But he didn't know how you broke into film, maybe you should ask around, somebody could tell you. Paul's own ambitions were limited. He'd never got his degree and now he was going to. He'd find a way to make a living without selling out. Such a sweet, no-bullshit guy, gotta love him.

Anyhow, during their conversation, it was hard not to get fascinated by one of the sculptures, a big metal thing that moved: two long silver needles pointing up to the sky, the fluffy white clouds there against a fantastic blue. But they moved back and forth, really slow, crossing and recrossing like scissors. Finally, Paul asked him what he was looking at but didn't quite understand why the sculpture was so interesting. At least he didn't laugh: he was a beautiful, sympathetic kind of guy, but was going to leave soon; it was in the cards, no way out of that. You can't count on anything or anybody sticking with you, it never lasts.

His neck is stiff, hurts to turn his head, and he moves his tongue around in his mouth, but it's dry and thick. Somebody's fingers run lightly along the scar along his clavicle, the welt he knows to be pink and shiny like cake icing. His first wound, and not all that serious. The stupid gook couldn't use a bayonet or he'd have aimed lower. Well, that stupidity had cost him his skin. Inevitably you looked at them after you took them out, it was the least you could do, a mental snapshot you'd carry with you from then on. His body sprawled, the mouth still open from the last yell, his little navy-blue cotton VC cap spilled on the ground beside him. About eighteen years old, young and inexperienced, but an ear is an ear, war is war, what the hell. The numbers racket. Thirty ears equals a three-day pass. So many offensives per so many days. Three wounds and you're out. They had a big, room-sized computer for it and made statistical predictions, which were sometimes on the money. But not always, everything would be reversed, the moving parts of the strategy wouldn't mesh, and the offensive would go bust. You started over from scratch. At least you had something to go on when the big brass ran interference for you, trying to foresee every problem, even though there were never any guarantees. And it was true about the ears, as he found out. The hard part was not to think of them as anybody's, anything that had ever been alive, not to take them personally. You stashed them out of sight until you had your quota. And only the left ear, only the left.

Carmencita always got down on her knees and prayed afterward, clutching the gold cross with its dangling chain in her long fingers. It had maybe an amethyst at the center, or piece of purple glass. She also had a black rosary and counted out her prayers on them. She said it was penance, and she knew how many to say to make it stick. He didn't try to stop her, but it meant nothing to him. Believe it or not, there *are* atheists in the foxhole, a few. And some of the best fighters because, like, they don't believe they've got heaven to fall back on if they fuck up the tactics and find themselves facing the business end of an AK-47.

S-2 worked out the figures, way up there in Army Heaven. Orders trickled down from the big brass, the division HQ, to the battalion, the platoon, on down to yours truly, the platoon leader, and then each man with his assorted hardware, along with the contingencies. Improvised strategy by itself couldn't come up with a plan that would do the trick with that particular configuration of hills and rivers. A grunt in the

49

field is distracted by the heat, the endless varieties of leaves and vines, all of them swarming with bugs and VC. It took the God's-eye view to translate that random confusion into clear-cut directives. S-2 worked out all the moves, came up with the best tactic for Hill 400 or Hill 937 and passed on their conclusions. Obedience jumped by a multiple with each downward link in the chain of command. The numbers were transformed into bombers, heavy artillery, and nighttime offensives, today F-4s, tomorrow B-52s, it was impressive to sit there and watch, cradling your M16 while the tracers zipped through the air like Morse code without the dots, the mortar fire doing its thing long about midnight, so your watch said. Fascinating to see all that algebra and calculus flaming against the blue-black sky. As long as you could think of it as abstract pattern, there was no problem.

Last spring had its rains. He began to get restless, but he didn't think he'd be able to get rid of Carmencita, she'd wound herself around him like a strangler fig. But he also in a way wanted her to stick around kind of, once Paul had gone, because there wasn't anybody else. He and she would stay indoors all day, laying around in their underwear on sheets that had gotten pretty damn funky considering nobody could remember to change them. She'd light two cigarettes at once and hand one over to him. Then the bitching would start, she'd needle him about anything and everything. That time he flicked the ash on her stomach, and she slapped him. Then she giggled like it was a joke, showing her two front teeth. Then she wanted to do it, but the sex part of it didn't work for him anymore. That wasn't what he wanted from her.

Paul and Carmencita had hated each other right from the get-go. He wasn't sure Paul realized she was a working girl. Paul was hard to read. You never could tell what his words really and truly meant. OK, it was clear he felt something, but what exactly? There was never any way to ask. And once Carmencita had moved in, that was it, he stopped coming by. Maybe if she hadn't—. Still, Paul was going out to San Francisco to enroll and get his degree. Even if he'd stayed in New York, would there ever have been a way to get across… what? Feelings and such. It would have been hard, and besides the habit didn't make you want to talk one helluva lot, although he got as far as saying, "You see, Paul, I've got like this habit." Paul didn't go for that at all, and apparently it didn't make any difference that the whole thing had started in an Army hospital. For Paul it was a sign of weakness, and as soon as what was happening began to dawn on him, he began to gear down, hold himself off. The guy was angry, and, on some level, hurt. Carmencita was the final deal-breaker. Paul said he'd call when he was settled in San Francisco. But he never did, never sent an address or anything. Well, still, he was one straight-up dude, nothing would change that, not ever. If you've been in the same platoon, that's for life, you'll always love the guy. Things hadn't turned out the best possible way, but hey that's the breaks. And the habit helped deal with it. People have different kinds of habits, and his was a fragile one, hard to manage with finesse, it needed a lot of supervision. His skin turned white and hard as plastic when he tapped on it with his fingers.

Numbers. He was the only one with a watch, so they would ask him what time it was. Everybody wanted to get the fuck out of Nam, they were sick to death of it. Three wounds and you're shipped. Which helped him do the kamikaze war hero thing, double or nothing. It worked. He didn't get himself killed, and he did get shipped.

The early part of last spring it rained, cool rain, not like the lukewarm showers Nam-side. He stumbled into a bar in the Village one weeknight around twelve, a dark place lit by flashing Christmas lights though it was April, and a little dance floor, with disco Top 40s playing in the background. There she was, one high heel dangling from a foot dangling from the barstool, lean as a whip, her hair pulled back in a long black ponytail. She gave him a look that dared him to ask her to dance, so he did. Even though he was already drunk on top of his fix. That was the start of it. Eventually she told him Carmencita wasn't her real name, but she needed it to be, so he didn't mess with her about it. She also said she was thinking of changing it back to Lourdes—she pronounced it *LOUR-dez*— but then so many people already knew her as Carmencita, they wouldn't cop to it. Later, they went out into the light rain, and neither of them had an umbrella, but they decided they liked the freedom. The cool feeling across his forehead like the damp cloth nurses sometimes ran across it in the Japanese hospital. Carmencita laughed and he could see beads of water on her hair in the streetlight. It was the high point, that walk home, that whole week, every day raining, but they went out for walks anyhow, Greenwich Avenue, Sixth Avenue, Carmine Street, Leroy, St. Luke's Place, all of them wet. He stared at vague jellyfish on the black pavement, no, larger, Portuguese men o' war, flat, rainbow-colored oil slicks, washed up and dead on the drying asphalt, now that the rain had retreated down gutters out of sight, rushing through the sewers toward the sea. Saturday of that week she said she needed to go back to her place, but before she said goodbye, she bought a bunch of violets from an old lady sitting on a camp stool outside the Eighth Street subway entrance and quickly pinned them to his jacket, pricking her finger in the process. She cussed and shook her hand, sucked on the finger, but then burst out laughing and kissed him. And that was it. She vanished below ground, an afterimage of dark eyes hanging in the air, nothing else, but seductive enough by themselves.

In actual fact, it came as a relief when they could finally do it. The thing they'd been trained to do from the beginning. Which built up a head of steam, pressure that only going the distance could release. Kind of hard to describe how much you need after a while to squeeze out a round or two. Hit something, anything. But that wasn't the whole story. Some of them had the real killer instinct, shit, they were up for anything. Way they looked at it, they were just getting a little payback for their buddies who'd been killed. The angriest fucks in the platoon became the interrogators. High in the air, copter blades dimming sunlight that streamed down on them and the green hills below, the new experts went at it. If they weren't getting anywhere, they'd slowly push the gook closer to the door, let him hang out, and if they still didn't get anything, give him a final kick out into space, hearing the last scream as he dived spinning toward the earth. Down there, off to the left, a yellow ribbon of road through the jungle, and you saw a puff of dust trailing along it from some jeep or truck on its way somewhere. Tank maybe. And the one left behind began screaming, they couldn't get him to shut up except by a rifle butt in the belly. The actual interrogation wore you down, exhausted, you just wanted it over with. Half the time you didn't know what the fuck the gook was saying, it was just a gabble of words and sobs, and it was hard to care whether you actually got any information or not. There was one, though, that never made a sound, no words, no whining, nothing. Soon as they saw he wouldn't sing, they kicked him out, watching as the body shrank in size to a tiny ball that plunged into the green. You couldn't hear anything but the chopper. And felt seasick.

He got Carmencita into smack, and then actually she used her own contacts to score for them, which saved time. The first time he shot up in front of her, she tried to appear jaded, said, "I know about that stuff. I got friends who are pushers." But she'd never tried it, not even to snort. Needles made her skin crawl; she never really got used to them. He could probably have gotten his hands on more high-grade medical apparatus, but the street equivalent was good enough. If you're going to be a junkie, you might as well go along with the crowd. At first Carmencita didn't get much out of it, except for the thrill of saying she'd finally gone all the way. But she caught on to it after a while, and liked it, especially after he agreed to fix her himself. Bad dope etiquette, but then he was in some ways an amateur, and what difference did it make, really. He could see her point, why she liked the attention. In the Japanese hospital, when the nurse arrived with your little hypo, it was like being at a ritzy restaurant and having the waiter light your cigar for you.

Sometimes sprawled on the bed to stare up at the blue ceiling is just like lying low in a trench, one bullet away from deep six during an offensive. But quieter, deader. He'd thought he wanted to rack up his three wounds, let them pin a basketful of ribbons to his chest and get the hell out of the war. It took him a long time to realize what was what. For two weeks he lay in the bed at the Air Vac hospital in Da Lat, leg in traction, the tubes, the paraphernalia of healing, the pain to study. He kept seeing an afterimage of the chalk-white bone sticking through the skin and muscle of his leg like a bull's horn. Gored with a compound fracture. No, he didn't realize at first that he'd miss it. Only later, at the

Japanese hospital, did it dawn on him. Too late. The magic of numbers. He'd gotten himself permanently debarred from participating. And he missed it, the completion of the circle. He felt bad that he'd left all his guys to fend for themselves. Half of them weren't going to make it, and meanwhile, you'd got yourself shipped, like you deserved something better.

In Basic, you said all the killer prayers, and you bayoneted the straw dummies, but you never actually got to do it. The pressure built up. So, when it came, what a relief. Finally, it was allowed. From that it was only a step to interrogation. OK, he couldn't do it, so what, but guys he loved could, and he didn't blame them. War is hell, it fucks with your mind. Sure, some of the interrogated were women. But women never told much, probably because they didn't know shit about what was going on. But they had to be questioned anyway, and that could get rough. Phosphorus. Plug-ins to the field batteries. They seemed especially afraid of knives. You don't forget that.

Saigon, well, a totally different picture. Everything was either/or. "You want number-one blowjob? Come on, you no want number-ten girl. Get very, very sick. I get you number-one chick. You not hap to pay." He kept wondering why the middle numbers were never used. A number-three blowjob might not be so bad. But it was one or ten. Three, four, five or six didn't mean anything.

Last spring he woke up thinking he heard the hiss of radiators, but after a couple of seconds he could tell it was the sound of showers outside, the Village dark and gray under rain. What has anything got to do with anything? He couldn't remember it all. Still, day did follow day, like a procession of solemn monks, hooded, carrying crosses and banners, you could barely see their haggard faces. The sheets smelled of mildew; Carmencita turned over and stared, waiting for him to show her something she could get interested in. Out of the pure accident of their meeting came an exotic flower made up of questions and answers, discoveries, pleasure and pain, a blood-red poinsettia that didn't match the Easter they spent together, Carmencita running off to her mass in a white shift, then throwing open the door when she came back, "ready for love," as the song on the radio said. The feverish scurrying under stale sheets that wouldn't have made any sense to those out there for the Easter Parade, already disappointed anyway by the rain, the gray avenues rainbowed with oil slicks. An Easter of sodden rabbits and pastel chicks dripping colored dye into the gutters. Afterward, Carmencita said some more prayers in Spanish. *Padre nuestro, Santa Maria....*

Granisin. He says the word aloud, enjoying the greasy sound of it, going back to laugh at the nuisance, a little payback from his Dominican sweetheart. But she swore she didn't have it. Maybe she'd taken a shot of antibiotic, he didn't know. It was true there were times when he blacked out for several hours and didn't know where he'd been or what shit he'd let himself be suckered into. So maybe Carmencita didn't have it. She complained for days about a burn she got while ironing a white shirt for him, chasing away the springtime damp from the fresh-laundered cotton. Fleeces of Easter lambs, gold crosses dangling on their chains.... A small scar formed on her wrist, pink and silky against her tan. She held it out for him to kiss and was even happier than before. It was so fucked up.

The girls in Saigon always confused f's and p's when they spoke English. One came up to him in a bar on Tu Dou Street. She was wearing a Suzy Wong dress, slit at the side, and she'd had her eyes cut occidental. Smiled at him and said, "Will you be my priend?" Sure, but since she was number-one it would cost him. Women had been dangled in front of the recruits starting with Basic. Everybody said it: When you get over there you can have all the gook women you want. Well, you could, but it was almost always a cash deal. Those women drove you crazy, the way they let you think you were the boss even if you weren't. It was all about money and hopelessness. Hard to get them out of your head. One who said her name was Nhu. After they screwed, and he was still lying on the bed naked. And she tied her silk scarf around his neck and told him to keep it. Which he did, he still had it. One thing he remembered from this past winter: He came across it in a drawer, next to his dog tags. So, he stripped, tied it around his neck again, and stared at himself in the mirror. She said her name was Nhu. "You puck me again, soldier boy? One time no good, we puck two time."

Paul thought they were great, too. He and Paul did the special-op stuff together, but when they took a break; they always talked about different hookers in Saigon or Eagle Beach that they knew. Or they'd talk about what they should do with Ferris, this other guy in the platoon who used to go apeshit when he was on leave in Saigon. He was a little shell-shook and probably ought to have been discharged. Right, but all the guys liked him, even though he drove everybody nuts. He had a way of imitating combat noises, sort of drove it into the ground. Like in the middle of the night. He'd wake everybody up and you weren't sure if it was a nightmare or what. He'd make this whistling sound, just like mortar fire, then the big explosion, *zee-ee-ee thump P-KROOM!* When they told him to cut it out, he'd just laugh and do it louder. It was nuts. But Ferris was a great guy, really funny, and not a yellow bone in his body. Too bad he had to go and get himself snuffed. During one of the ops west of Cu Chi—no, Phu Lo or ... Damn if he could remember now. Well, anyhow, Ferris used to go on these sex binges in Saigon, all the girls knew him, he was a good customer. And a pothead, but who wasn't.

It took Carmencita a while to get anything out of smack, but she eventually did. Made things easier. Some night in early June, wasn't it? With summer coming on. She sat there on the bed for a long time, looking surprised. She said, "Yeeaahh. All *right*. O-*kaaay!* What's happening!" She repeated that. Now she understood, and so he wouldn't have to go on feeling like a freak. Later, she began to rap about her childhood, what it was like for a little kid with a mother but no father in Dominica, poor as dirt, in a shack with a dirt floor. And she knew she was better than that, her grandfather had owned horses at one time. Then her mother got sick, she couldn't take care of the children so they were sent to their grandmother. Abuelita was soooo good to her, but then she died. She prays every day for Abuelita, every day. So Carmencita got sent to New York, her aunt and uncle took her. They lived up on Nagle Avenue in Washington Heights. Now that was a big change for a kid from Dominica. The Big Apple, and she was maybe ten years old, hadn't learned English yet, so school was way too hard for her. Besides that, she didn't know to watch out and be careful, and one day when she was walking in the park by herself this big guy—really big, oh man, he was a giant!—jumped her. That was the start of it. Eventually her aunt and uncle kicked her out, but by then she could take care of herself, girl, don't you worry. There is always money for any little mama who knows how to take advantage of the situation. From the first she knew what was going down. Just don't fall in love, that's all, because love is bad for business. "But now I *have* fallen, with you, baby daddy, which is why I don't have no money anymore." She laughed. "You know, you got to cash these disability checks, they just sitting here." He promised he would soon. He said he'd give her some pocket money, and she kissed him.

Then she closed her eyes and started praying. When she stopped, he said, "Spanish people are more religious than Americans, aren't they?"

She didn't like this. "I'm an American. I have citizenship. But yeah, you guys don't believe in nothing, I don't see how you live that way. You better watch out." The insulted queen. He nodded and took hold of her chin, his thumb rubbing her lips, which seemed to soothe her. She went back to her childhood in Dominica. A little skinny girl who used to take walks by herself. Out in the wild part there was a big black rock right next to a stream, with green plants growing all around it. She would sit down and look down at the water, and there was her reflection. So sad. Some other kids came by one time and pointed at her and made fun. "Lourdes, Lourdes, little frog, sitting by the river!" But she didn't care. They didn't know Lourdes was an angel, an angel who had fallen down into this world. And they never would know. Then her grandmother took her away.

Saigon had a few things going for it, but he didn't like all of it. Wooden balconies that overlooked twisting back streets. Bars and women, pimps, young boys in dresses and makeup, not that you could always tell. They flirted the hardest, and some of the soldiers went with them as a kind of joke, like it proved they were even more macho than the ones who were afraid to try it. Which made sense in a way. Pot sold on every street corner and they all smoked, but you had to be careful not to get too stoned, you might forget which was your ass and which was your elbow. The heat was the same as out in the jungle, the bugs were the same, the bony faces were the same; but here they weren't the enemy, you had to remember that, you had to hold back your reflexes, stuff that'd been brainwashed into you as far back as Basic. Officers seemed able to manage that, but some of the grunts ignored where they were and got in big trouble. So, you had to watch out, keep your head fairly intact. He'd copped his thirty tickets, earned his three-day pass, and all he wanted to do was forget the whole goddam mess. But you had to keep your cool. He took the money he'd saved and bought a good watch. That helped keep him grounded in reality, which there never was much of in Namland. He could say no to the pimps on the sidewalk, the number-one girls in the bars. But Nhu had persuaded him.

By the time he realized he didn't want to go, it was too late, they were shipping him. The people up in Army Heaven computed he had earned a Bronze Star, a Purple Heart or two, hell, a Presidential Citation. He thought he might as well wear the ribbon as long as he was in uniform; but everybody had it, they were all decorated like Christmas trees, what was the point. Brass handed out medals like jelly beans. That was supposed to make up for all the shit. When he got to New York he sold them. It paid for a couple cartons of cigarettes. Checks hadn't started coming and he was hard up. Anyway, it was a big mistake to walk the streets in uniform. People said and did every fucked-up thing, including spit at you. You could say, "I went to Vietnam because, one, I was drafted, and, two, to save all of you from Communism." But you knew saying it wouldn't do fuck. Lot of them *were* Commies or least wanted to be.

Carmencita couldn't believe her luck. She always loved big blond hunks, she said. It wasn't hard to understand, she was dark, and the men in the bathing suit ads and cigarette commercials were always blond. Opposites attract. "A working girl is the opposite of a soldier, am I right, huh?" She laughed at her own joke, lit him a Marlboro and sat there thinking about something, holding the cigarette between thumb and index, her palm tipped upward, a ribbon of smoke floating toward the ceiling. When they fixed, she would talk softly, squeezing the eye-dropper. Her face was lean, bony, her hands too large for the rest of her, a light silt of makeup on her face. She always pronounced b's like v's, and vice versa. One of her pet words was "emvarrassed." So many things "emvarrassed" her. The outfits people in this town wore were so emvarrassing, they have no taste. She didn't like Ricans at all, the way they acted was emvarrassing. "Dominicans and Ricans don't get along," she explained, and she listed reasons for it, first, second, third, fourth....

She loved to put him on, and when he snapped at her, she would shrink back and widen her eyes, pretending to be terrorized. Somehow, though, she always knew when he was really mad, and those times she melted into adoring softness, kneeling at his feet, stroking his hand. He would be sarcastic for a while, then eventually calm down. He would smile at her, his eyes brushing up and down her body. She said, "Oh, Mike, baby, you're emvarrassing me!" And begin to purr. He knew she didn't mean it; it was a come-on. And she would start needling him, like always. And so on, until he hit her. That was the drill.

After she picked up the habit, though, things began to change. They spent whole days just sitting around, and she didn't seem to need to do much more than that. She would stare at the works—the spoon, the eye-dropper, the spike—and that was enough to occupy her mind. Or she would tell him about growing up in Dominica: it was paradise, except they were poor and the other kids made fun of her. She would sit on the floor, the lamp behind her, her face in profile, dark, with a silver rim, like the dark of the moon. An hour could pass. Then she might get up and turn on the TV. They'd watch anything, it didn't make any difference what, they were above it all, but enjoying the irony of it, the smooth, velvety way the smack made you see it, the soft-grained texture of the images in black and white, the closeness and the distance. "This is nice shit, isn't it?" he said. And Carmencita nodded slowly, turned her face away from the TV and looked at him, a gentle half smile overtaking her face. Because now they had something in common, as they'd never had before. "It's divine, *amor*," she said, "divine." So, there was no real need for sex, it had been obsoleted. They'd run out of ideas, anyhow, done about as much as they could get up to along those lines. But they had dope now. Which would coast along for a couple of hours, and sometimes the channel they were watching would sign off with brass bands, spangled banners furling in the breeze, the black and white stripes reminding him of convict uniforms. So, they'd be left behind staring at the snowstorm that boiled inside the tube and listening to the white noise coming out of it. Maybe that was best of all, no pictures, no words, the meaningless flow of electrons, the way reality truly is, deep down there on its own level.

He needs to make a decision. He needs to throw all the chips up into the air and let them settle, pick and choose. Which part of the evidence is useful and which not. He has to decide and the fever in his chest plays a part in that, right along with the time of day. How much more does he want to learn about all the flavors pain comes in, and will cold turkey have anything new to teach him? He's been through worse; it might include new information. A line of thought that doesn't really fit in with all the memories, the mosquitoes lighting on your arm and pumping away, the sound of the chopper blades, the violets pinned to your jacket, rainbows on the pavement. No way to resolve it, make the kaleidoscope shape up into a plan, life doesn't give you your own private S-2.

He remembers the summer that came in, hot and dry after all the spring rain. The cleaning woman banging her bucket outside the door as she mopped the landing. Summer called down the fire-escape, trickled in at every window. The heat bitched on every street corner. They stayed indoors with the air-conditioning, going out once in a while to cash a check, score, buy cigarettes. At least you could get takeout just by telephoning, which saved a lot of effort. The Chinese delivery boy would catch a glimpse inside the apartment and hurry to get away as fast as he could, the door slamming behind him. Footsteps, rapid, retreating, and then gone. Mostly they just picked at the food, not really hungry. It was like getting C-rations, you were eager to open them but then you didn't really want them. Looked like it was going to be a long, hot New York summer, and what they heard was the air conditioner, which they never turned off, its low *whoosh* reminding him of driving at night with the windows down, air streaming through the car, rushing in his ears. It covered up thoughts, helped you forget all the things you've done. Until you remembered them again. Remorse, that was the operative word.

The commanding officer never mentioned what happened the *last* time they tried that un-routine tactic in one of the ops, now that they were going to try it again. Orders were computed by S-2, and that settled it. So, they pushed ahead through the thick bushes and vine-strangled trees, even when any moron would know trouble was on its way. He did and didn't get used to seeing shiny, green tropical leaves, just like the ones you see in a florist window, but with blood on them here. If you got it on your hands, it made them slippery at first, then sticky, and it would get on the gun, too. And it stank, you couldn't wait to wash it off.

That silver sculpture in the museum garden, one of the best moments he and Paul had had. The silver needles swayed with the breeze, pointing up to the sky with it clouds like torn-up Kleenex. Of course, the idea about making a film hadn't gotten anywhere. It was just a fantasy. Like hoping Paul would stay with him and not buzz off to San Francisco. It's fucked up when people leave you like that. He'd gone with Paul to the airport, even if his buddy wasn't really comfortable with him anymore. A hug, a goodbye, then he said, "Write when you find work." But Paul never wrote. The end. Finito.

The whiteness and the cottony texture of cotton batting, the dressing on his leg. He'd been bedridden for a month in Osaka, and twice a day the Japanese nurse brought him a full hypo. She seemed very different from the gooks, and he understood she was off limits, most likely. But she would look him in the eye, and her own eyes were nice, they hadn't been Westernized. The sheets whispered underneath his fingers, soft, chalk-white, clean. And when the rush came it was like sailing through feathers or clouds, flying through the TV screen after signoff, the grain of it, the white noise, cool, serene as air conditioning. All the programs finished. And summer heat had dried up the men o' war from the pavement, leaving a film of dust behind. All burned away.

One day, when they were fooling around, he had tied her up. But then he realized it wasn't such a good idea because of course you might get carried away in the excitement of the moment. Besides, why tie someone up when what you actually wished was, Christ, that she would go away and leave you the fuck alone? But not really. It was too late; he didn't want to get rid of her. Thing was, they never should have gotten together in the first place. Because after that, Paul didn't want to hang out with him anymore. That ship had sailed.

And so, then, one day she cashed in, an OD she had set herself up for, even though she didn't like needles. Her final courteous gesture to him was to do it in the park at night. Her courtesy to herself (he guessed) was that it would take a while, as she had come to realize. That left her a few minutes for her prayers. He didn't like thinking about her kneeling under the trees and, at some point, slumping to the ground. Didn't like that. No way. But then he was a shit, right, bro? And addicted to shit. Anyway, when they found her the next day, nobody would connect them, he wouldn't have to deal with formalities, not to mention possible arrest. It was written up in the paper, otherwise he might not have ever figured out what had happened to her. She slipped out after he'd fallen asleep. He found her note the next morning but all it said was, "I love you, baby." So why did she do it? He knew but he didn't want to say. He was pretty sure he fucking knew. That day he'd been talking about Paul, what good buddies they'd been, so close, and he wondered if he'd ever have a friend like that again. Carmencita looked up at him and said, very slowly, "I will never matter as much to you as him, will I?"

He blinked at her, turned his palms out, shrugged, and said, "It's a different kind of thing."

"Thass exactly what I'm saying. But it's more like it than you want to *admit*, baby." He shook his head, but he didn't actually speak. And she lay face down on the bed and didn't ask him any more questions.

The point was they had been together so long that anything he said, any decision he made, involved her, too. Weird, but the fact was that skinny little Dominican had a thing for him, and here was one more thing to feel guilty about. The price of kicking would be, you'd have to think about things. But he *already* was failing to avoid that. Already was thinking. For example, he realized he never wanted to see Paul again, Paul would not ever be the same as before. So, sure, everything and everybody was already stirring around in the pot together, and, when he decided, she'd be involved in the decision. A fallen angel sitting on a black rock in Dominica. Number-one angel. The hands of the clock had met at noon now, clasped together like hers when she prayed. Forgive me, angel, forgive the habit. Who knows why, she took the gold chain with her, but she left behind the big cross with her note. Steps outside on the landing. They clacked ten times, then they died out. Rain beginning now to fall on the streets. The note was signed "Carmencita," as would be expected; but then that was crossed out, and under it she had written "Lourdes."

He's Funny That Way

That I both did and didn't want to go to San Francisco only added one more conflict to the chaotic swirl of emotions surrounding a departure date. I'd agreed to do a teaching gig there because funds were running low, and Gene was between acting jobs (nothing new in that). Besides which, he grew up in California and feels expatriate boosters of the Golden State should revisit it every year. Four months away from home is nothing, really, but my New York parochialism always asserts itself before we take any trip. I have this funny, unexplainable reluctance to deal with. Dread and queasiness lead people (like me) who are normally easygoing to behave badly. We pitch hissy fits with people we love and concoct insults that never would have crossed our lips if we didn't have a thousand practical telephone calls to make or several hundred pounds of sundry schlock waiting to be loaded into the car. Past experience had taught my main-man Eugene that, when those moody winds swept in, anyone within range better watch it, he was in danger of sustaining blows about the face and eyes. Lucky for Gene, he also knows how to dodge and feint like a Kung Fu black belt and, what's more, to land a few pulled punches now and again.

Another convenient brunt for my bad temper was Teddy, our doorman. Hefting the unwieldies out of the elevator so I could load them in the car, I lobbed several tart comments his way, at which he grinned his idiot grin—one corner of the mouth going up, the other down—and said nothing, the most likely method of squelching the tenant confronting him. On a blazing day in August he should have been overheated, too, in his tight-fitting gabardine uniform (Teddy is fat) and cap. Oh, no. Unflappable efficiency kept opening the door of the air-cooled lobby and sending this hapless Okie tenant out into the swelter. As much as I'd let him, Teddy would help me with the bags, somehow never losing his baby-elephant complacency. My physical clumsiness, which I try to see as an endearing fault, today felt like one of the afflictions visited on poor slobs that Miss Happen Stance likes to oust from their comfortable slots—why? because she gets bored, wants to be amused, and thinks a homo on a hot tin roof would make an interesting spectacle.

Gene and I had never lived in a doorman building before. Here's how it happened. An older well-heeled friend of ours named Ralph Dunhill, who has several chi-chi addresses scattered around the globe, when he heard our apartment building in Chelsea was about to succumb to the wrecking ball, offered to sublet us a co-op he owned up on the East Side (at a nominal rent) until we found a new place. Was Bette Midler ever right when she sang, "You got to have friends!" There was just one problem: after plumping ourselves down at Ralph's, we totally failed to find new digs so that we could move out again. Our gracious living requirements and our bank account were singing in a different key. Actually, they still haven't managed to play in tune, so we've come to regard the clash and jangle as modern music. We looked and sniffed and turned down everything in our bracket that was shown to us. Our interim sublet continued on and stretched out into a residence pure and simple. Ralph didn't seem to care. Those times when he wanted to spend a few days in the city, he stayed with us. No longer young himself, he was nevertheless (unheard-of trait) a fan of youth and beauty. But he didn't like going out to trawl for it. We'd invite a few studmuffins from our gym over for dinner to meet charming, silver-haired Ralph. Some of these, as we'd guessed they would, turned into projectile rent-boys at the mention of a London flat or an April jaunt to Sicily—the usual upshot being that a match for the night or the month would be made. Everybody came out ahead, whether on the giving or receiving end.

When we first settled in at 77th Street, we congratulated ourselves on the new perk of enjoying doorman service. It was nice to have a soft-spoken, efficient man in uniform take your packages, send visitors up after a polite intercom message, and whistle down a cab when you wanted one. Actually, there were three, two reliable elder statesmen to handle these tasks, and then Teddy, the younger, less formal third. Though none of them really approved of us, not even Teddy. Quite clearly, we didn't fit in with the genteel atmosphere of the building, wearing jeans and even Ts, our guests in equally informal attire. It takes an experienced Eastside doorman about five seconds to decide whether you own municipal bonds or not. Gene and I sometimes came in carrying plebeian sacks of groceries, whereas the building's "nice" co-op owners had theirs delivered—through the service elevator, of course, according to civilized practice. Furthermore, although some few of the other residents were secret friends of Dorothy, our behavior was way too "out" to suit the tone of this particular enclave. Gene and I pretended not to notice the ironic smiles that went with the elaborately polite words greeting us as we waltzed in and out of the lobby every day. Despite which, Teddy began to cross the invisible line that protocol establishes in such situations. Given his obvious conviction that we had no class whatsoever, why did this one doorman want to be friendly? We didn't know, but he clearly was angling to punch through those ice curtains his co-workers always closed against us. It made for a pleasant contrast. I mean, at first.

"Now when do we expect you back, Mr. Caswell? Early December? I'll mark that in my book." (The one formality Teddy stuck to was the "mister" bit, which was even more preposterous than usual, pronounced in his museum-quality Brooklynese.)

"Right, and if you'll just hold the junk mail. Thanks, I've got this one."

Heat volleyed up from the pavement and glared from all the black and silver cars double-parked on 77th Street, including my Stratus, which needed a wash. I unlocked it and threw in an inordinate number of bags, the question of whether we'd need quite so much paraphernalia flashing through my mind one last time as I tried to fit everything in. Then, right behind me, up stepped my hubby, a freshly pressed Empress Eugénie, with his little black duffel, plus picnic basket with a carefully

67

wrapped bottle of Prosecco protruding from it.

"The duffel can go anywhere, but why don't we keep this within easy reach." He put them where he thought best, returned my do-what-you-want-to-sweetie look with a snippy smile. A lean, blond icon in sunglasses and sandals, he's an object lesson on how to be sultry-sexy at thirty-seven—which probably explains why he has the upper hand in our particular tandem. All I ever need do in order to push myself into a stimulating episode of self-denigration is look at us side by side in the mirror. It's not possible not to wonder what he sees in me. But I don't *ask* him because the question might introduce a hairline fracture and break the spell of downwardly mobile enchantment. Renewed awareness of my amazing luck, of the imbalance between his visuals and mine, didn't, even so, help me get a grip, not at that moment. My cool cucumber of a spouse turned and walked back to the door being swung open for him, me muttering under my breath and following after.

Thanking Teddy, Gene swirled around toward me, flipped off the sunglasses and said, "Listen, Matt, I'm going to telephone and say goodbye to Ralph. Do you think you should stay down here and keep an eye on the double-park?" It wasn't a real question so I didn't answer. The *clip-clap* sound of his sandals on the tiles as he walked to the elevator reminded me of summer a year ago in Greece, where he'd first bought and worn them. Now that was a trip. We *were* capable of having a good time together. Today, not. I slouched down on the lobby sofa. Through the grillwork shadows of the doors, it was fairly easy to make out the car. Nobody likes waiting, but at least here inside you had shade and A/C to assist while you cooled your heels.

Teddy was my junior by about seven years, a fact no more reassuring than the thought that most policemen are younger than I am now. Authority figures, people in uniforms, should be as old as your father, or so an ironclad sense of suitability tells me. Teddy was the same age as my kid brother. And since most of the building's tenants were in their 60s or 70s, an odd complicity had grown up between him and me, as representatives of a newer crop of humanity. Eventually though, I began to discourage the chummy tone. The tack I usually took was to breeze past each morning's fresh-served joke, nod, and then stride forth into imperturbable sunlight. Once, when Gene and I were going out together, Teddy gave us a leer and said (to the partner he figured as the "woman"), "Oh. Mr. Downey, are you carrying Mr. Caswell's baby?" His double-barreled "mister" in the context of pregnancy really pushed the envelope, but that's our boy. I glared at him and said, "Drop it, Teddy," flicking him off my lapel, so to speak, like a crumb of pizza crust, as we fled the precincts and set out in search of company less crude. But that was then; on moving day, the routine M.O. didn't hold. As long as my loaded car was double-parked, Teddy had a captive ear for his ready wit.

Which he figured out immediately. Eyes dark brown and face round as a mushroom cap, he approached me, his fists dangling at his sides. "Mr. Caswell, did I tell you about my aunt?"

"Did you?"

"My Aunt Martha died. This is the one my mother didn't speak to anymore. Well, because: One night, this was back in the Fifties, before I was born, they was going to a New Year's Eve thing, a big fancy party over in Kew Gardens. Like I said, I wasn't born yet, this is like my mother telling me the story. She got all dressed up—you know, she had on her fur cape with the squirrel heads biting each other—and they drove by first to pick up my aunt. Mother took one look at her and says, 'What'sa matter, your lipstick is crooked.' And when Aunt Martha tried to answer, my mother says, 'You're drunk, Sister.' Didn't I tell you this? Aunt Mart was really kind of plastered already 'cause it was New Year's. They went ahead to the party anyway, and at the party they had some kind of party punch with vodka and cream de cocoa I think in it. So, it was party time, and my aunt drank a lot of the punch and started asking all the men to dance. So, finally, my mother said we're taking you home, and then Aunt Martha insulted her, and—"

"Hold on a second, Teddy, they're going to give me a ticket." I went out to the curb and talked, in that volcanic heat, to the unconvinced young woman in cap and uniform. The car would have to be moved. Now. No ticket, just this once, but I've been warned, so get moving, sir. I circled three blocks up and down and then, the meter-nazi having plodded farther along on her daily rounds, slid into the same exact illegal space. But Gene still hadn't come down.

Almost before I was inside Teddy restarted his story. "So anyway, after Aunt Martha insulted her—"

"Um, Teddy, let me phone upstairs." I did. On the house intercom our voices, staticky like cellophane. Gene had been comforting Ralph, who wanted to communicate the news that his mother had gone into Intensive Care. Ralph was devoted to his mother, so his trip to Finland and St. Petersburg would be a no show. Gene had done his best to find the right assurances and was sorry he'd taken so long. If I could just be a little patient, he'd be there in a jiff. The first thing my eyes alighted on when I put down the phone was Teddy's face, brimming with narrative lust.

"So anyway, Mother wouldn't speak to her after that, not until she apologized for saying what she did. Except that Aunt Martha never would apologize, she just moved out to California—this ain't where youse guys are going, it was L.A. But nobody had her address, and they didn't know what she was doing out there anyways. But then my mother got word from a mutual friend that Aunt Mart was dancing in a nightclub show. See, she'd always been very talented, she could sing, and she'd taken tap and modern. Aunt Martha was the kind of person she always got a kick out of showing off for people, like, at parties and things. Mother claims I take after her." Teddy laughed, both pleased and self-deprecating, then went on. "But Mother was like real upset when she heard her very own sister was performing in a nightclub, to her that was just like if she'd a been a—a criminal pervert. And she felt guilty about it, like maybe she was partly responsible because Aunt Mart might not a gone to L.A. if Mother had stopped speaking to her so nasty. You know what I'm saying?"

"Excuse me, Teddy, I want to check something." I'd seen a delivery van backing up to the car. I wasn't sure if they were going to block access, so, safer to ask. Out into the furnace. I went around to the driver and talked to him and his assistant. They scratched their beards and said they'd appreciate it if I could back up, say, a few feet. There was a furniture delivery for the Josephsons. The seventh floor, was that right, did I know? I said I thought it was, moved the car, and stepped back into the lobby, my hands sticky from the steering wheel. Cool air washed over me.

"They want to make a delivery, Teddy."

"Oh? OK." He looked outside to where the two men were wrestling a big carton out of the van. Then he turned back to me and picked up his thread. "So, my mother felt guilty, and then she felt even *more* guilty, you know why? Because one day she went out to the cemetery to put flowers on my grandmother's grave. It was Gamma's birthday. What she found when she got there was, Gamma's tombstone had tipped over flat on the ground, face down. She got to thinking about it and figured it was my grandmother being so upset about what happened to Aunt Mart. You know, from beyond the grave. *Woo.*" I saw a shiver run through Teddy, then he recovered and plunged in again. "My mother felt so bad about it, she got, *man*, like, real sick. The doctor put her to bed for two weeks. And she got my aunt's address finally and wrote her. She told her she was very, very sorry and would you please come home. But Aunt Mart never answered. Never heard a single word. And after a while the family lost track of her completely and just gave up trying to get in touch."

He scuttled over to hold the door for the two deliverymen, who were piloting a big brown cardboard box into the lobby and then back to the service elevator, toward which Teddy shepherded them in a series of flitting but authoritative gestures. By now I was curious to know what had happened to his aunt (such is the tyrannical enchantment of story), and when he came back, I asked him.

"I was going to tell you. See, last New Year's my mother went to another party, also in Kew Gardens. A different house this time, but just like before, a classy level of people. Actually, she said a few of the same guests were there as at the other party, just kind of discrepit now. A lot of them had died since the first party. Anyways, just as they were about to leave the party, my mother had a mental experience, like. She heard a voice that was saying her little sister would be dead before next New Year's. And she busted out crying right there. Because she and her sister had been real close when they were kids, it was only later they

71

got sore and stopped speaking to each other. So, my father asked her what was the problem, but she wouldn't tell him, so he thought she was having too many cocktails. He said let's go home, Tess. And she didn't even tell him what it was until last Friday, when they got the news."

"You don't mean your aunt died."

"Yeah, Aunt Mart was dead. And some friends of hers got in touch with us."

"I'm sorry."

"Thanks. I didn't really know her, she left before I was born, but she was a terrific person, and she was my aunt, so I loved her." We blinked at each other silently.

"I'm going to call upstairs again," I said.

Gene came down. We said goodbye to Teddy, who waved from under the awning outside. At some point during his story the car had been ticketed; there was the slip under the windshield wiper. I released an appropriate profanity. Gene let this dereliction of duty on my part balance off his dawdling upstairs. As we buckled ourselves in, the delivery men came out of the building, visibly thrilled to be free of that heavy appliance or whatever. They looked at Gene and nodded goodbye to me. They must have figured out that we were (to borrow a 1950s bit of gay slang that Ralph pipes up with occasionally) "as queer as Dick's hatband." One of the men started whistling like a canary, the other one volleyed a gob of spit into the gutter. (But don't they always, the cold war among demographic categories being what it is. Say what you like, none of us passes for straight when sized up by construction workers and delivery men. They seem to have better gaydar than the middle class. Oh sure, I realize that their gestures are as much come-on as insult. But my tactic is always just to whistle back even louder and let fly my own gob, so that they know I'm not fazed in the least.)

As we thrashed our way through traffic toward the Lincoln Tunnel, I began to retell Teddy's story, which at least got us out of our grim, set-jaw mood. There was also the relief of finally having got the trip underway. Oddly enough, during the week-long drive, Teddy's name kept cropping up, for no special reason, in a thousand haphazard contexts. And because that old standard came on the radio one afternoon while we were analyzing his weird, moony innocence, we started adding the refrain, "He's funny that way." It was almost as though he became the mascot of the trip. "He's funny that way...." Some of his choicer comments have entered the private, ironic phrasebook that every couple develops over the course of their years together. For example, whenever we get gussied up to go to some fancy soirée, one of us usually says, "Now don't forget to put on your fur cape with the squirrels biting each other." And so forth. Of course, Teddy's contributions amounted to only a small percentage of the rococo lingo and wry inflections at our disposal, but still.

As I mention this, it occurs to me to wonder why it is that folk on the gay side of the fence develop and deploy so much special idiom while working out our aberrant destinies. I specialize in interior design, not sociology, but I can theorize that we use clever verbality as a first-line defense against... well, you know, all the walnut-brained lunks who think they've pronounced words of thundering originality as soon as they've called us fags. We tweak and hone our blithe condescension and stiletto putdowns as a way of proving, if only to ourselves, I AM SOMEBODY: tony bitchery as self-affirmation and survival technique. And once we've seen how effective it can be when used on the dire straight world, we can then direct it at our own kind, staging a festival, a reciprocal orgy, of personality roasting. Put two or three Queer Eyes in the same room and within six minutes at least one of them is going to have his beads read in agonizing detail. Do I need to point out that we're all capable of aiming the same Star Wars ray guns at ourselves while we're at it? Why else do we all strive so insanely to be flawless on every front? If we weren't perfect, our Inner Mommy Dearest would reach for her correctional coat-hanger and get to work.

Anyway, Gene and I beguiled the long hours of the driving day by retelling all the old stories from our pasts, interjecting an occasional Teddyism for comic relief. As soon as the drive was over, though, we relieved our daffy doorman of his tour of duty; and never thought to call him once while we were in San Francisco.

* * *

73

Now it's December and our West Coast interlude is over. We've been driving the reverse route back through all kinds of weather, and I'm ready to resume my former existence—as much as anything future can be former. As we turn onto 77th Street, Gene gives me a quick, excited smacky. The city's been subject to several transformations since we left. The air is cold, it's night now, and all the avenues are blaring with the lit-up fanfare of the last few days before the chimney-drops begin. From a dozen apartment windows on our block half a dozen Christmas trees in silver tinsel drag are winking and flashing their sugarplum-colored lights into the darkness. We slip on our jackets before beginning to unload. Who should come out to help us but—our very own Teddy! Strange, because he never works the night shift. But he's been transferred—at his own request, he tells me, when he shakes my hand.

"Welcome home, Mr. Caswell, Mr. Downey," he says. "Just in time for the holidays." Well, sure: He's due his bonus check any second now. You can see, though, that he is sincerely glad we're back. And I feel a helpless, sickening rush of homecoming warmth toward him as well, which I *will* overcome eventually, just not tonight. Cooperating, we get everything smoothly into the lobby. Gene surveys the pyramid of boxes and bags and says apologetically, "Hope you can manage this. I'll put the car up." He twinkles a "ciao" at me and steps outside.

I'm waiting for our 1930s-vintage slow-boat elevator. Shaking his head at our "stuff," Teddy catches me by the sleeve and brings me up to date on the building gossip. Until I interrupt him: "How's your mother?"

"Oh, well, she's getting along OK. She and my dad are going downta Florida right after Christmas Day."

"You're not going with them?"

"No, it's not my vacation. I'll stay and take care of the house. While they're gone."

"Won't that be lonely? But you can throw a big party." *Bingo*, Teddy blushes a big bright red, and it's obvious that I'm on target about his plans.

"Mother wouldn't like that, not in her live-in-room. She'd be afraid of cigarette burns on the live-in-room suite." But practiced detective skills tip me off that he's just going to ignore those restrictions and throw his party anyway. We're looking in each other's eyes; he knows I know. Wait a minute, is that—? Yes: He's exuding a floral-musky-roach-spray aura. No, it can't be, but it is: Aramis. (I have a Proustian flashback to 1975, an era when the little tot I am knows something is *different* about himself, just not what exactly. A little tot who can name any perfume he smells.) There's more. Teddy's left ear now sports a little gold ring. Aha, bet 77th Street doesn't like *that*. Now what do I imagine he'd say on being asked, "Oh, Teddy, have you gone gay since we left?"? A plan I instantly reject. He's sure to say YES, and then we'll *really* be defenseless against those volleys of sassy cheer delivered in the lobby every evening. I will happily join other building residents as we muscle him back into the closet, at least for the hours when he's on company time. (With a certain amount of concern in his voice, Gene will report, a week later—the morning after Teddy's unauthorized winging out in deepest Brooklyn—that our debutante has a black eye and a cut on his chin. But that will be only the beginning, only the beginning....) At last, here it is, the slowest elevator in captivity. It opens, and, as I step into it, Teddy beams his big, space-dish grin at me and waves, "Merry Christmas, Mr. Caswell! Happy New Year!"

Irish

Periods. We should have visited them in chronological order, but flight connections call the shots, so the trip began at the end with Dublin Airport (Modern Period). Our United jet landed as an Aer Lingus jet took off. The signs in the airport alternated English and Irish, as though the mixture were the most obvious and natural thing in the world. Dublin itself was a patchwork of jumbled eras. The view from our hotel window alone spanned probably two centuries, up-to-date commercial carnival on Capel Street shading off to the Four Courts' Georgian aplomb—anyway, enough to make us hanker to get out there and see it all. Because you're as hardworking a vacationer as I am, we absorbed the sights in just a few days, even so leaving plenty of time in the evening for the highest-rated snuggeries (Edwardian Period). It would have been criminal to miss them, considering that local whisky, knocked back in the right company, confers honorary Dublin citizenship. Resulting warmth in the gut is happy to meet the glow coming through the next pair of etched glass doors (and the next) pushed open in the new citizen's serial pub-crawl.

Once the lovably shabby capital was absorbed, we had our backways and sideward itinerary to follow west and south, which would take us through the epochs, eventually arriving at prehistoric dolmens and mystic rings of standing stones (Neolithic Period). Our marked-out territory explored, it would then be time to come full circle and drive to Dublin again for the flight back to New York.

An oddity about touring around in other countries is that the proportion of brute fact to direct experience suddenly doubles. Places, dates, the names of important but obscure bigwigs—all that sweeps aside the obstinate tragi-sitcom of home. The gospel according to Baedeker takes it for granted that tourists can transform by some sort of alchemy the gobbling up of landscapes or monuments into a pilgrimage and possibly even a pivotal chapter of their own personal history. And why not, since so much of what's in theory private actually occurs in public. Case in point, that incident at Cashel (Norman Period), where I made the wrong remark to you and got told so, at top volume. Innocent enough: I just said, "Well, if you'd stop nursing that half pint and get your nose out of the guidebook, we could actually go over to the castle and have a look at it." Which earned me an "asshole" and a few other hallowed abuses. Afterward, we sheepishly promised to avoid staging a scene like that again in front of astonished locals; and most days stuck to the agreement, at least halfway.

The project wasn't high on the list, but we hoped there'd be a chance, when we got down to Cork, to make a two-hour detour and visit one of the Great Houses I was curious about. Ireland has them to burn, you said. Sure, but this particular G.H. had two distinctions: A famous Anglo-Irish novelist grew up there; and it has disappeared. Not because the house was one of those that perished during the Troubles; it came to a more prosaic end. This writer had left it early in life to go to London. You said that was very bright of her. Anyway, when she began publishing, people praised her fine-grained perceptions and style; but then the Anglo-Irish thing began to fall out of favor. Childless, and never a best-seller, she couldn't justify the expense of maintaining the place, so, in the early Fifties, up on the auctioneer's block it went. ("Her version of the best-seller" as you remarked.) A prospective buyer materialized; she met with him and his family; liked them; and told herself the house would be in good hands, its long, mirrored halls echoing with laughter as adorable, knee-high futures scampered through them. But no: All business, her buyer just wanted to cut timber on the property—why, who'd ever dream of living in a white elephant as drafty and unheatable as that? The eighteenth-century structure did have one valuable feature—the leads covering its roof. So, he tore it down and (the businessman's version of alchemy) exchanged the lead for a pot of gold, which was a sight better odds than the Sweepstakes. You interrupted to ask whether we ought, seeing that we were here, buy one of those tickets. I dismissed that and went on with a narrative it was clear only I cared about. I'd been trying to make my point: All the ex-landowner could do was write a memoir about the ancestral manse (Georgian Period) and cross her fingers that at least its quintessence had been distilled and bottled, in her perfectly calibrated paragraphs.

I'd thought we might at least want to see the *site* of the house, the place where it had been remaindered and then pulped. I say "we," but it was probably more my idea. The marital "we," already reacting to travel stress, had by then totally broken down, alternating between silent freeze-outs and some godawful exchanges. The words "fucking idiot" were used a couple of times, OK, but not by me! Understated digs are more my specialty—along with considering severe critiques re my character or fundamental value as probably accurate. Which is a grave mistake, even if the critiques *are* accurate. But there I go again. Wimp.

Bicker, gawk at scenery, bicker, gawk: Our running quarrel flickered on and off like subtitles to a foreign film. It was one more strain to manage, along with sitting behind the steering wheel on the right and driving in the left lane. One of us we's was having to do exactly that every day, as required by law in all four corners of those isles that used to be called British. I suppose a little love-candy from time to time would have helped. Mornings, though, we were too bleary from the pub of the night before; and, evenings, too exhausted to launch into one of those hot parts foreign films are noted for. During the day, we were traveling, so, in effect, our trip had made celibates of us. At least you kept your sense of humor, though not everyone would have recognized it as that, I mean, given the acid content. Example: You thought I was a touch too proud of my ancestral connection to the Old Sod, and, after I'd mentioned something about forbears in Armagh, supposedly the blood of kings, you said, "Oh, stop putting on Eires—E-i-r-e-s, get it?"

I winced out a smile and said, "Got it. I mean, I wasn't claiming that the line didn't also count a few itinerant tinkers and spud farmers." At least your joke had defused a little tension. Which is what wit is good for; that, and sparkplugging the front lobes of the brain. What it doesn't do (too competitive) is create warmth and solidarity in the first place. And yet I never wanted to be one of those people who say, "I know I'm not very smart, but I am good-hearted." As for warmth, we'd always found that whisky helped. But then it wears off. Might our nerves not already be a bit on edge that very morning? If so, who could blame them? Nothing but coffee at breakfast to fend off the hangover, with the result that the day had a buzzy, headachy tinge to it. Green fields, green trees, and green hedges flew past, green as love, green as envy, green as jealousy.

It wouldn't be accurate to claim our behavior was peevish or pettish or waspish merely because we were traveling. Duking it out—and then trying to determine who was or wasn't to blame—counted as a notable feature of life back home. A feature or even a fixture, and the same goes for the unofficial (but hardening!) habit of joint celibacy, less and less often violated over the past couple of years. A friend suggested couples' counseling, but I winced at the prospect of having to hear the phrase, "failure to communicate," not exactly news, and as such liable to be greeted with a choice horse laugh from your corner. The defining moment, the one that said it all, had come a few months earlier. I'd stalked into the living room of our apartment, bent on reporting, *that very second*, an earthshaking discovery. You were fiddling with our temperamental FM, clearing up the sound as an announcer droned on in resonant tones about some music program that was going to alter the course of history. But that didn't seem any reason for me not to blurt: "Listen, I think I've figured out why, for two whole months, we've been at each other's throats."

The last word wasn't out of my mouth before you said: "*Sh-h-h.* I want to hear who conducted this performance." Eventually the name "Christopher Hogwood" or "Neville Marriner" was announced, I don't remember. After which, you turned around and said, "OK, so what is it?" By then the sheer pointlessness had come as clear as stereo, and I let it drop. I lack perseverance; but then how could True Confessions compete with Mozart's *Sinfonia concertante?* Besides, music criticism was what you did, it's who you are. You *had* to hear that name.

"I think we turn right here. This red road." The map rattled in my hands, a multicolored meshwork of highways and byways printed on folded pleats.

"But that would be going *west.*"

"How do you know?"

"Look where the sun is, dummy."

"It's overhead—well, almost. I can't tell."

By making several wrong choices that cancelled each other out, we eventually reached our destination. The road rises up to the top of a hill, then you turn into a sandy track and stop by a sort of gate house, new, not old, where the grounds-keeper lives. Predictably, not home at the moment.. The boy standing at the partly opened door was his son. In the adjoining meadow, crickets busy rasping hind legs together filled up the pre-social silence. We hinted we'd be interested in seeing the estate. No problem, he could show us around. His blue eyes gave out the flat, unsuspicious stare of the countryside, beamed from a face, pale and on the good-looking side, under a nest of tangled brown hair. And immediately joined by another face, fresh and pink, belonging to a girl who said, "Hi," then, "Shall I go *with* you, Kevin?" She didn't look like him; and the teasing was too intimate to be sisterly. "You might want your cap, love, heat's fierce today."

But Kevin decided to manage without it. We all four walked together along a path overgrown with weeds. Feeling expert, I put in, "Those are nettles, aren't they?"

"I wouldn't know," Kevin said.

"If you touch them, they sting."

"Really?" He reached out and brushed his hands through a feathery tuft of them. "Yeh, they must be. Where are you from?"

"New York."

He brightened. "I knew someone who went there once. You've got the Hard Rock Café, haven't you."

"Um, yeah, I *think* it's still there." He looked at me, then away. Briefly impressive, I'd revealed myself as totally out of it, and my novelty value plummeted.

"You came all the way *here* for your holiday?" There was as much contempt as disbelief in that "*here*." But, when we admitted that we had done just what he said, country tolerance (Early Medieval Period) shrugged and tolerated. But maybe it was time to shift the focus from us to them. Kevin answered more than half of the impromptu interviewer's questions, and the girl, whose name was Kate, the rest. They were going to be married in October. There was plenty room in the gatehouse, so they could live with his widower father. Kevin would take over the grounds. Once Kate was living with them, they would let go the Mrs. who cleaned, which would be a savings; she was ready for retirement anyway. They'd worked out everything in advance: in life you just have to lay your plans, it'll be grand.

"You've got to have a positive attitude," Kevin said. Information and philosophy were conveyed in perfect trust that listeners would, first, grasp relevant issues, and, second, would care to hear. One reason, probably, for the steady flow was the fact I'd let drop that my great-great-grandparents had emigrated from Ireland (Potato Famine Period). Like, we were practically kin!

People sharing ethnic ties nevertheless retain the right to change the subject, so I said, "The old house was torn down before you were born, right?"

"A long time before. I never saw it. My Da remembers it. One time they invited people that worked here up for Christmas Eve and gave them all a present." This was said without enthusiasm or envy. "He told me it was grand. I don't remember what the present was." A stick Kevin had picked up along the path waved in the air and then came down with a neat whack at a tuft of nettles.

I asked if people hunted on the property nowadays, and he said they did. Fox-hunting? No, more like deer, in the autumn. No horses involved, just people trying to put meat on the table.

By now the path had opened out into a field planted in rows with something dark green and low-growing. Asked what it was, he said,

"It's beets. The owner plants them every year. Easy to grow. Sugar beets. Not for eating."

In the distance I made out a dark-gray, walled-in roofless rectangle, too small to be ruins of the house. No, it was the old garden, still standing—but with a wide breach in its wall. We walked up and noticed the original wooden gate, rotting, hanging sideways by one hinge. A peep inside revealed more beet rows. But the tops of the walls were overgrown with ivy, collegial ivy, ivy so thick someone would have to have pruned it, back in the heyday. But when was that, exactly, 1750? 1890? There was probably more than one. A closer look inside turned up what looked like a fig tree in a shadowy corner—but no figs, so maybe it was some other tree, also fruitless. Partly hidden by its leafy branches, a damask rose with four or five pink blooms climbed the wall. In the month of May, young women let out from the G.H. would have bent to sniff them, on their guard against the thorns.... Otherwise, nothing now but beets, as far as the vegetable kingdom was concerned. I stooped down and fingered a crinkled young beet leaf, pale green with a red central stem. It could serve as a little botany lesson, putting aside its agronomic, commercial context altogether. The root was certain to be sugary-sweet, but the leaves—one of the trendy new salad greens—would have a nice bitter tang to them. A sudden twinge in the gut reminded me I hadn't eaten anything today.

Then something glinted. On the ground next to the plant, half buried in sand, was a fragment of ceramic. Even before picking it up, I could tell what it was: Delft, small blue flowers painted over a white background. Reunited with its scattered fellow fragments, it would have made up the sort of bowl or jug that catches morning light in a Dutch painting—an illusion so entrancing viewers will sell every tulip they own in order to buy the work it appears in. So. The free-of-charge relic went easily into my pocket.

You asked Kate where the house had stood. "Em, I'm not sure. Kevin? They want to know where the house was."

He steered us out of the garden. "Over there. Between those trees." The looming absence was marked by two tall evergreens, an uncommercial species worth less than hardwoods that had been cut elsewhere on the property. We paced the area between them, overgrown as it was with grass and nettles. No souvenirs for the taking here. We'd heard birdcalls earlier, but it seemed to me that they stopped for a minute, replaced by a solemn, cricket-chipped stillness. To stand there without moving was a brief furlough from any hard and fast identity. How to name a contentment based on being a mere perceiver, uncritically taking in the scent of warm grass, the specific, floating gravity of the clouds overhead?

Contentment has a way of yielding to other things, though. I pulled out my pocket notebook and began jotting down a few words. *Sugar beets ... walled garden*. Note-taking was a habit of mine you didn't have a lot of patience for. Fussy and plodding both, you probably thought. (But writing is what I do, it's who I am.) This time, too, you grunted and turned aside. Which may have been the jinx that made the pencil-lead snap off in the middle of a word. The projected travel article I hoped to produce, as a way of paying some of the expenses, would have to depend on mental notes alone; so it might not get done at all. And that would be too bad, because one of our conflicts was that I didn't earn as much as you did. Granted, I *tried* to, but the market for thoughtfully phrased perceptions is what it is. Ask the former owner of this ruined estate. Idiotic, bringing a pencil rather than a ballpoint.

Bored with standing around, Kevin said, "Want to see the chapel?"

"What chapel?"

"Well, you know, they weren't Catholic. They had their own chapel. It wasn't torn down."

"Oh. Sure, let's see that."

We walked back in the direction we'd come, the youngsters striding ahead of us. It sounded as though they were quarreling now, too. You and I were sort of walking on eggshells and hadn't said a cross word to each other for an hour. But maybe even an unspoken mood is catching, almost certainly it is. Kate's voice went up in an intense, high-pitched whisper, only a few words reaching us farther back: "... *not* going to ... Why do you say that?" Well, the sun was hot for this part of the world, and the Irish, bless our genes, do get angry. Kevin whacked at the green wayside weeds with his stick, but then Kate suddenly grabbed him around the neck and kissed his ear, unselfconscious and entirely in love and twenty years old. Sweet. I shot you a look as a way of saying, "Well. What about those two?"

But nothing had prepared me for the look on your face. For once, the ironic guard was down, and I was staring into the eyes of a ten-point stag with a dripping, red bullet-hole in his side. Why? And why just at that moment? Unanswerable. Blame travel disorientation, the angle of the sun, the spectacle of young, uneroded romance skipping along the path ahead of us. Stag image aside, I think it was the first time I'd actually *seen* you during the whole trip—the red face agleam with sweat, the trimmed, salt-and-pepper beard, the thin hunched shoulders, the fists dangling at your side. A body always makes an impression any time we do take the trouble to notice. Whatever it was, quick as a reflex, my own walls, walls of an interior city (Feudal Period), tumbled down. I wanted to make you feel better; and feel better myself because of the day's Good Deed. If Kevin and Kate hadn't been close by, maybe we'd have said something constructive. But not just then; we weren't going to go public with it all. Weird enough already that two grown men in beat-up Nikes were tramping around a beet-field like old marrieds, mooning over days of yore. Or one of them, at least. I didn't know what you felt. Later on, the moment had passed; a brisk, intelligent tone returned, more familiar and, frankly, easier to manage.

The chapel was no longer used. Once every few years, on Christmas Eve, a parson from the county came over to conduct services for a few local people. Dead leaves, perhaps a dozen of them, lay scattered over the floor; damp, mildewy smells shadowed the air. A sad, religious absence, old as Ireland's mystic stone circles, commanded the space all the way up to its dark-beamed roof. Our novelist would have, presumably, been christened in that font near the door. Had she also been buried from this chapel? I didn't know her story well enough to answer; or enough about Church of Ireland liturgy to be certain its requiems back then would have included a *Dies irae*. Probably not; even the Catholic church has dropped that.

Kevin and Kate were standing up front, back-lit by afternoon sun filtering an array of pastels through the one stained-glass window over the altar (Victorian Period). I imagined seeing twin disks of light around their heads, gold as the wedding rings they'd exchange a few months from now, though not under these Protestant beams. Anyway, they weren't still snapping at each other; in fact, Kate was giggling at some joke or out-of-bounds squeeze of Kevin's. They strolled down the aisle toward the rear, passing me going in the opposite direction. I came up beside the old pump organ, whose cover was open, exposing the keyboard to dust and damp. Scattered on the floor beside it were several pieces of ivory that someone had ripped off the keys and tossed aside, just for the hell of it. The damage hadn't been repaired, which meant nobody really cared. Anyway, the temptation was too big, and here came the day's second larceny, this one (bless me, father) committed on consecrated ground. I bent down and picked up one of the ivory pieces, slipping it into the same pocket as the ceramic shard. Guilty as charged; but on the other hand, neither item had any monetary value, right?

The Delft bit seemed worth keeping—and, in fact, has jogged my memory, a replacement for the notes I didn't take. The piece of ivory, I gave to you a day or two later, during our drive back to Dublin. Granted, the timing could have been better. I was driving, and that always brought out your inner control freak. The radio was on; I was humming along with a cut sung by a rock group called Savage Garden. When you complained about the noise, I groped in my pocket for the ivory and handed it to you, without explaining why. And the gesture must have left you ... mystified, irritated? Looking at the little white rectangle in your palm, you only said, "What am I supposed to do with that?" I couldn't see my way to answering with the kind of wit you'd respect. So, I took the little keepsake back, rolled down the window, and pitched it out. The speed limit was no object as we drove down that left lane in County Cork, so it's easy to imagine that piece of litter spinning through the air to hit the shoulder at sixty-five kilometers an hour—decapitating a dragonfly in the process? There, among the nettles and shamrocks, the little key is laid to rest. *Horseman, pass by!* Now that our biographies no longer overlap, at home or anywhere else, I don't really need it in order to get my point across.

MARS

Though we met the day after I signed the deed for the Fifteenth Street apartment, Steve and I didn't get to be close friends—at least, before his bad luck got underway. He was just the six-foot-two guy with the boxer's build who lived next door. Our bedrooms shared a wall, my side of it a glaring bone-white I soon painted café au lait. I seldom saw my neighbors and never tried to know much about them, partly because they didn't try back; but, just from surface clues, I gathered Steve and I were the only gay men on the sixth floor.

The Wednesday after moving day, my snazzy or dubious belongings still stacked in the living room, I rang Steve's bell, hoping to borrow a hammer. We'd only just said hello in the hallway the day before, so I hadn't really had time to size him up. When the door opened, bang, there he was in a tank top and shorts, as if he'd been expecting a visit and wanted to bring forward his strongest assets. But how could he have known? He couldn't, so I guess he was, like a good Boy Scout, always prepared. He had the sort of ringletty short hair that doesn't need supervision anyway, though just possibly it had started out in life a different color from its current chestnut brown.

As his good deed for the day, he volunteered to help me hang pictures, and during the measuring and eyeballing and hammering process, which got the supersized and handsomely matted photographs relocated where they'd look best, we began to exchange verbal résumés. Corporate accountant? Certainly not built like one. Meanwhile, he sounded sincere when he said it was cool that I was a photographer and that he loved the shots we were putting up on the walls. I liked his hoarse voice, a little higher pitched than you'd expect, and with a Midwestern accent describable as corn-fed if you wanted to be condescending. As soon as it was clear he was unattached, I made sure to tell him about my recent breakup and having to leave my partner's place down in the Village. By then I'd developed and rehearsed a standard rap about it being a smart move to have my own base of activities for a change, you get so tired of compromising with another person's living habits. Also, I wanted to see if what people said about Chelsea was accurate— in theory, the neighborhood of choice for up-to-date single guys who had begun to move there in the late Eighties and celebrate the end of the Reagan era. A celebration that automatically assumed his White House replacement was going to be an improvement.

My casual suggestion that we go for dinner he accepted innocently, without a smirk or a missed beat. The apartment was still a mess, so I was eager to spring myself from it for an hour or so, and have a quiet, maybe spicy meal somewhere. Although, in fact, Chelsea isn't so sold on being quiet, and instead of spicy we ended up with Italian. Walking back to Fifteenth Street, mellow from a shared bottle of cabernet, we decided not to end the evening just yet and have another drink, but indoors. Remembering the miscellaneous heaps of whatnot all over my three rooms, accidents just waiting to happen, I asked if we could do it at his place.

He'd painted his walls gray and everything looked as impersonal as a hotel lobby, the expensive dullness only emphasized by track lighting. He had no photographs or paintings, just nicely framed reproductions of garden-variety images like Van Gogh's *Sunflowers*. I drifted around, pretending interest in the surroundings, swirling my wine in its big globe, while he made unsurprising comments about this or that piece of furniture or knickknack. In the bedroom there was a picture not as quickly identifiable as the others, an Old Master portrait, mythological probably, of a bearded man, wearing a helmet and holding a sword. The posed military figure's torso was bare, and looking at it you registered that the model wasn't young, distinctly weathered and wrinkled— odd for a classical subject. I waved my glass at it and said, "What's the painting?"

Steve looked at it, paused, and then said, "I can't remember." He took it off the wall and turned it around, read the label and then said, "It's *Mars*, by Diego Velazquez. It's not a real painting, it's a reproduction."

"Oh, I knew that. But … you liked it because he's … sort of a warrior, is that it?" We stared at each other longer than the standard three seconds, Steve the first to blink. It occurred to me that he was a little older than I'd guessed. Also, that, as a follower of the Chelsea age code, he probably considered himself on the verge of obsolescence. The picture must be an early warning to anybody who made it as far as the bedroom that they weren't going to get a specimen of rubbery youth. Myself, I never insisted on flawless stats; to me a little age isn't a bad thing at all. Anyway, be here now! Drink up! I put down the glass, closed the short distance between us, and managed an approximation of a bear hug. He accepted it, but then, after a few exploratory clinches, stepped back and said, "I don't think we know each other well enough yet."

True enough, but knowing each other better probably wouldn't add much to the skin-deep scenario already in play. Mere animal magnetism ought to be enough for uncomplicated, short-term liaisons. Bruised by my recent breakup, I wasn't in the market for anything serious yet, so uncomplicated, skin-deep overnights suited me just fine. But what can you do, we were one short for tango: I backed off and said I should be going. Steve walked me to the door and before it closed flashed some nice dental work when I said "Ciao."

Over the next two weeks we met several times, shared a couple of meals, and did some more fumbling, even a little snogging. And yet never quite got to the point; so, bar by bar, the original electric fire faded and cooled. Steve became just my neighbor, someone I spoke to when we happened to be riding the elevator together, or traded jokes with when we were both watering straggly evergreens on our adjacent balconies. Judging from thumps, groans, and loud laughter heard through the shared wall of our bedrooms (shoddy modern construction practices!), he seldom spent a night alone and clearly didn't need to worry about being carded for having gone over the age limit. When you have quick black eyes and a square jaw like Steve's, heightened by the correct amount of facial hair as dictated by this year's trends, and when you faithfully do your lifts and reps and the stair machine, Chelsea offers dozens of daily opportunities. For an impressive number of people, those opportunities make staying at home with the other member of your civil union look tame and sleepy, as, to be honest, it is in many ways.

My long effort at exclusive partnership had come to an end the year before partly because we'd both found a typically suburban substitute for mutual monotony. That didn't mean the omnivorous approach felt natural and easy, not yet. There was no doubt I was overmatched in singles skills by Steve. OK, but only in that one field of endeavor. I'd put him in the category of the likable but not over-bright; realizing of course that his type usually does better in the quest for good times than the minority I belonged to—the ironic, the over-thoughtful, the chronically dissatisfied. Anyway, the work I was doing, which had moved away from photojournalism into something more like art, was beginning to get recognized. So professional success took up the slack from any self-doubt I might have felt from failing to market myself effectively at the bars and clubs. Let him enjoy his butterfly existence, I had my Lasting Contribution to make.

These self-bolstering terms of comparison didn't prepare me for the seriousness of the conversation we had about five months after I moved in. Late August rain had been coming down in gallons and kegs, blown sideways by winds sent up from the latest Gulf coast hurricane. We both lunged into the lobby at almost the same moment, shaking the water off our umbrellas, which were still dripping when we stepped into the elevator. During the ride up, he sneezed and said, "If you've got a minute, do you want to have a drink?"

"Uh, sure. Mine or yours?"

"Mine, I've got this." He pulled from his shopping bag a fifth of Laphraoig.

Sipping his shot glass a few minutes later, he put his stocking feet on the coffee table and said, "Got some bad news today." Another sip and then, "They did some tests at the hospital. There's, um, you know, a tumor."

My eyes widened, but I tried not to sound alarmist. "Oh. I'm sorry. That's really ... disturbing." A little smile twitched at the corner of his mouth but he said nothing. So I pushed on with, "But they've got fantastic treatments these days, really sophisticated operating techniques, and then of course chemo, et cetera."

"It's in the liver."

"Oh my God. What do they—" Steve just looked at me.

I guess this counts as the watershed between the old and the new Steve, I mean, my before-and-after sense of him. When I asked if he'd called his family, he said he hadn't. His father and mother both had pronounced some sort of DIY excommunication of him many years earlier, when he'd made his "coming out" phone call. He was still in touch with his sister, but it wasn't a close relationship, and he hadn't contacted her yet. Apparently, I was the first person he'd come out to about the cancer, a forthrightness that made me uncomfortable. It struck me that he never mentioned having any close friends. He had swarms of meetups that lasted for a night, but no one ever asks for a second audition in this part of town.

Why didn't I ask myself if I actually *wanted* the responsibility of being his "contact person"? Just didn't; and soon became Steve's sole channel of communication to the outside world. Within a month, his disability insurance kicked in, and, either because he didn't have the energy or else the ambition, he stopped going out. The bedroom wall was quiet—no, not entirely, once or twice I heard low-pitched groans seep through it in the dead of night. He had meals delivered and anything else he needed. I'd hear the pizza or Chinese takeout delivery guy ring his bell around 6:30 every evening. About three times a week I would ring it myself. Sometimes I'd knock gently instead and wait the minutes it took for him to slide out of bed and stumble over to let me in. Eventually, as he got weaker, he told me that the lock on the sliding glass door to the balcony was broken and that, if the bell didn't get an answer, all I had to do was step over the iron balustrade separating us and come on in. I nodded but said I was sure it wouldn't be necessary—a lame response, just what you'd expect from someone with zero experience in talking to the terminally ill.

At first, I avoided thinking the word "terminal," but after a couple of months there was no way not to. Because Steve hated hospitals, he worked it out with his medical advisors that he would stay at home. A full-time caretaker was arranged, and on his first day of duty I was invited to meet him. A man about thirty years old, Sudanese he said, very well groomed, and speaking enough English to do his job. It was the era when many gay men, because of the epidemic, ended up with caretakers, and the odd thing is that all those I ever met were invariably African, a fact I've never heard explained.

Once Yoel (that was his name) was in place, no doubt I could have, without a bad conscience, stopped looking in on Steve so much. But it seemed to me that I ought to do it *more*, to make sure he was getting good care. Even though my intuition was that Steve had had good luck in finding Yoel. Times when I did drop by, the apartment looked tidy, Steve seemed to be comfortably tucked in, and, if I asked him how things were going, he'd make a hand gesture signifying he was fine. Accepting his self-estimate required overlooking the fact that he was bone thin and had jaundice; but he was clean and so were his sheets. I considered it outrageous how his family didn't visit him, not even his sister. He himself didn't react when I said that, just half shrugged and stared at me with his dark, glistening eyes. To judge by the surface, he didn't seem to need comforting, and as the weeks trundled on, I began to feel useless, maybe even a little bit of an intrusion distracting him from an important job he had to do.

The one thing I was faithful about was taking Steve's mail to the post office, and the snoop in me noticed that there were never any letters to family members. No, except for bills, all the letters were addressed to charitable institutions, and you didn't have to be Sam Spade to detect that they contained checks. In neat, accountant fashion, Steve was distributing his material wealth, and not only to organizations devoted to cancer research or the Red Cross, but other groups I hadn't heard of. He'd been doing research, finding charities not especially well known that might need donations. Looking at all the envelopes, I began to feel selfish and tight-fisted. I even wrote a few checks myself to some of the more interesting organizations.

One Saturday noon during a lunchtime visit, I noticed that there was now a rosary hanging from the bedpost and well within his range of vision. For the time I'd known him, he'd never mentioned going to mass. However, once a Catholic, always a Catholic, even when you're an atheist. Sometimes I wish I'd been brainwashed into being a believer, but, no, my family was secular; for us, all religion proved was a failure in education. Besides, you'd have to get over the prejudice that kneeling and opening your mouth so that a disc of white stuff could be stuck on your tongue like a postage stamp was in bad taste. Even so, here's a scene that keeps coming back to me: a discussion we had one night about the afterlife, with Steve telling me I was dead wrong not to believe in it. One way or another, we were all going to resurface on the "other side." And that in some big or small way, we all do survive death. I could see he thought I was trivial-minded or soulless. OK, but soulless comes in different packages.

The letters (and disbursements) stopped when Steve became too weak to lift his hand to write. No more than a week later he went into a coma, as Yoel told me when he answered my knock. I asked if I could see Steve, and with no hesitation he took me into the bedroom. Steve was clean but motionless, his breathing audible. Everything in its place, the sheets, the comforter, the rosary, the bedside lamp, and the picture of Mars. Steve was still alive, but the thin face and shrunken limbs made him look like someone mortally wounded, left behind on a battlefield after the shelling has stopped and the troops have gone off with their loot. Too bad I hadn't given him, while he was still conscious, a last hug. Now the gesture was pointless and, besides, with an outsider there, it would have felt—I don't know, self-dramatizing or something.

I dropped by the next evening and made another five-minute visit. Looking at Yoel, I sensed his fatigue. The kind of vigil his job forced him to keep, even though he'd had a lot of experience, made me cringe, just to think of it. Also, I'd noticed that every time I looked in, there was an empty pizza container in the kitchen. Fast food is only bearable for a couple of days in succession, after which it becomes prison fare. It came to me that I should make Yoel something to eat. I remembered a recipe for a North African dish that used chickpeas and root vegetables, spiced with saffron, cumin and cinnamon and not so difficult to prepare. I had those ingredients and nothing on for the evening, so I revved up a George Michael album and got to work. Rattling pots took my mind off the negative aspects of the situation, and the result was soon ready.

Yoel hadn't expected me to knock again. When he opened the door, he looked at me intently and then at the plate I had in my hand. I said, "I brought you this, in case you're hungry."

His gaze flicked back and forth between my eyes and the plate, but then he took it from me and said, "Would you like to see Steve?"

We walked into the bedroom lit by the one lamp and now very dim. I sat down and looked at Steve, whose mouth was partly open, breathing, breathing, breathing. Yoel said, "Is not going to be long time." The impartial finality of expertise. We sat and then I urged Yoel to have his meal, otherwise it would get cold. Reluctantly, he stood, went to get a fork, and began eating.

"Your family is in Sudan?"

"No. They died. After I left, my town was … attack. Soldiers kill everybody. You have heard of this in Sudan?"

I nodded. "That's terrible. I'm so sorry. Really awful." He didn't lift his eyes from the plate. We sat in a silence broken only by Steve's breathing. The lamp seemed no brighter than a candle, the rheostat must have been turned down. There were shadows in the corners of the room, but at least they didn't move, as they would have done in candlelight.

Yoel had finished about half the plate but then set it down and said, "I will have rest later." He looked at me and then stood. That was my signal, so I stood, too, and said I had to be going. At the door, I turned and saw him still standing and looking at me.

A restless night, so I was glad I didn't have any assignments the next day. The shoot for *Details* was scheduled for Friday, but that was three days off. I just puttered around, opening and shutting cabinets and drawers, trying to clarify my thoughts about what was happening next door. When the bell rang, I instantly knew it would be Yoel. Recessed lighting in the hallway ceiling marked out his face as a high-contrast study in planes and shadows. He held out the oversized white plate I'd given him, cleared of its meal now and apparently washed and dried. "Thank you, was very good." He said this in a voice not much above a whisper, in the slow, rounded Sudanese voice that had made a strong impression when we first met. Again, I noticed the truthful eyes, the finely calibrated gestures, the strong body that stretched the material of his white cotton shirt. After a pause he said, "This morning Steve have pass away."

I shook my head. "Oh God. Would you like to come in?"

"Well, for a minute I would like."

He didn't want coffee or anything else, so we lowered ourselves into armchairs, Yoel's eyes ranging around the room at random. New York apartments not in the luxury category are small, and there wasn't much to appreciate. Once seated, Yoel and I were less than a yard apart. "Did they call for the—did they pick Steve up yet?"

"Not yet. Later today, they say. I have address of the funeral place if you will want it." His fingers dipped into a shirt pocket to pull out a card that he handed to me with something like a flourish. I glanced at the sober print and slipped it into my pocket.

"I never go to funerals. I used to, but, then, after I went to, oh, it must be over thirty of them last year, I decided that was enough. It's been the Year of the Memorial Service for me." He looked off to the side (probably not understanding) and then down at his lap. "I think Steve said he was in touch with his sister?" He nodded. "Though not his parents."

"I don't know."

"Uh, I just wanted to say thank you for taking care of Steve. You did a wonderful job, and I know he was really grateful." (I'm a joke at making appropriate serious speeches.)

A silence, and then he cleared his throat. "I thank you again for the food." He was standing and holding out a hand, soft and dry to the touch, powered by his impressive arm. Our eyes met and sounded each other out. But the gloomy circumstances put a pall on things, and I took my hand away. I saw him to the door and closed it after him.

My apartment, with its geometric rug and Aalto furniture looked empty and chilly, even though sun was pouring in from the sliding glass doors onto the balcony. Most likely Yoel would be leaving in an hour or two and we'd never speak again. The naïve side of me dislikes to the point of queasiness these brief acquaintances, exchanges that seem humanly authentic but then come to an end with blank abruptness. People are brought into accidental contact with each other, there's something like minds touching, a sensation of friendliness and respect; and then both parties are swept away toward the rest of their lives. It happens all the time in the city, but it's not a topic I've ever heard discussed, so maybe I'm the only one that's bothered by it. My hand rummaged around in my trouser pocket and pulled out the card. I was going to throw it away, and then I noticed that on the back of it, written in careful block letters was YOEL, followed by a telephone number. Huh, isn't that interesting....

At some point just before nightfall I heard people in the hallway, voices, the sound of something metal, wheels rolling, Steve's door open and close. I was tempted to step outside and have a look but then thought how unpleasant gawking is to people on the receiving end. So, when Steve's door opened again, I didn't move, instead just imagined visuals to go with the sound outside—some sort of gurney with a body bag on it, men in dark clothes moving slowly toward the elevator. In less than a minute everything was silent. I must have left on one of the taps in the kitchen because I could hear a trickle of water running into the drain. Turning it off was at least a distraction, but as soon as that was taken care of, what next? I made an experimental effort to cry and got nowhere, just some hoarse breathing. Tears are one more capacity that's been shed somewhere along the road. I console myself with the thought that at least I know what I should feel, even if expression is blocked.

I hadn't met Steve's sister, all that he'd told me was that she didn't care for his "lifestyle." Even so, there was some sort of minimal communication between them, and I assumed she was his heir. Before long she'd fly into the city and come to clear out the apartment, a huge and hellish chore, because he had a lot of stuff very little of which she'd probably want to keep. For no real reason, I hoped he'd thrown out the porn movies, etc. After sifting through his drawers for valuables, chances are she'd hire someone to just empty the place. And that thought led to my little … infraction, my petty larceny. I went out onto the balcony and looked around. The afterglow of early evening still shone behind the black outline of surrounding buildings. One leg, then the other went over the balustrade separating my balcony from Steve's. Fearless Captain Marvel walked to the glass door, tugged, and, sure enough, it slid open.

Though everything was dim and still, the rooms felt (I knew this was only a feeling) inhabited. Instead of indignation, the surroundings gave out a sensation of, what, modest welcome, as though curtains and unlit lamps and sofa were saying, "Good, I'm glad you came." There was Steve's empty bed, stripped of its cover. And above it, the picture of *Mars*, which I could barely see, though well enough to go over to it. I caught either side of the gilt frame, lifted slightly, and took it off its nail. Not heavy, and not the least of an encumbrance when I stepped back over the metal bar separating our balconies, the lime-green arbor vitae brushing my leg as I passed.

Back inside, I put the picture on the floor, leaning it against the wall. Steve's battered old veteran. No need to decide instantly where to hang it, that could wait until tomorrow. But I was determined to put it up somewhere among my own photographs, those that Steve had said were So Cool. In the interim, I'd acquired my own hammer: no need for a second theft. And I had plenty of nails. Bang, bang, bang. There. Job done. Picture's up. Embarrassing bad taste, but *Mars* had found his place of honor, a décor mismatch not worthy of my stylish neighborhood. I could already imagine what friends would say. Depending on how close we are, I will or won't tell them the story. As for Yoel, if he ends up seeing it, I'll explain. I'm pretty sure he'll understand. Think of all he's seen in his life. He'll get it. Soon as I work up the nerve to call him.

AND QUEEN ANNE IS DEAD

He'd said, "A U.S. citizen can have two passports," but didn't know what she meant when Philippa, laughing with her mouth closed, followed up with, "And Queen Anne is dead." He figured his Yank naïveté was being made fun of. The British probably were not smarter than Americans, but certainly better with words.

"What's Queen Anne got to do with passports?"

"Oh. Sorry. It's an expression used when someone says something that's already well-known and obvious. I forget why. I think Queen Anne died—you don't know who she was, do you, Mark—but it was kept secret for maybe a fortnight, and then, when it was finally announced officially, everybody already knew. It's nonsense." She laughed again and her brown eyes wheeled as they always did when she was trying to conceal a superiority she didn't think she ought to feel.

He gave her credit for trying; and accepted it as, what else, a sign of the L-word. Think of that: for some strange reason she did have this thing for him. The "Honourable" title in front of her name hadn't stood in the way, no more than being English and rich had. It took him a while to catch on that setting her sights on him was part of a larger plan. She wanted to ditch her upbringing and be free of demands that went with it. Was that all there was to it? Maybe not. People said he wasn't bad-looking. Also, Nigel being his buddy. He and her brother had met in Afghanistan during a joint raid on a village in Helmand Province, Nigel a paratrooper and himself a Marine. In the burned-out aftermath they'd developed a friendship based on joint disillusionment with the war. A favorite subject was the chronic problem of "friendly fire" between Brits and Yanks, which had done almost as much damage as the Taliban. When they compared notes about their lives before combat, you got the ridiculous contrast between an American kid raised in foster homes he hated and a titled family's eldest son who kind of liked him. They sat on two facing footlockers for hours, stewing in their sweat, trading jokes and stories. He learned a lot about the English, in their way just as strange as the Afghanis. Maybe there was more interest on Nigel's side, a personal no-man's-land it wouldn't be a good idea to explore. But in the following months they exchanged updates electronically, which he could handle. When leave came up, he was invited to spend a few days in Derbyshire and didn't refuse. He'd never been to England but decided not to be intimidated, even to exaggerate being a Yank. Which may have been partly why Philippa warmed up to him.

After he heard news about the failed mission, the one Nigel didn't make it back from, Philippa got in touch and wanted to know if he'd be willing to come to Derbyshire again. Given the situation, there was no way to refuse. Anyway, the invitation reminded him that he liked her. Liked in a way that made no sense, considering her family. She wasn't movie-star glamourous, instead, impressive, in the way some women in law or business are. When she looked at you, confidence looked at you. Sometimes something scheming slipped into her eyes, but more often she softened it with a crinkly smile. If she got started talking, it was pointless trying to interrupt, she just kept going. You really didn't want to get in an argument with her. But he figured out that her secret wish was that she could be different from that, be open-hearted and yielding. He guessed that her clothes, frilly and weird, were planned to make her seem girlish, less intimidating. Once or twice, he heard her mother say something gently mocking: "Oh, look, Pippa's got a new dress, one of those designers, I expect."

It'd begun on that second visit to Belfort Hall. Philippa had taught him to pronounce it "Bevvut," which was nuts, but who was he to question it. He'd given the gathered family an edited version of what he'd heard about the mission that got Nigel killed and another one that got himself wounded in the leg. Philippa hung on every word, and so did her softspoken parents, whose shock registered as an intake of breath and an occasional, painful "Oh." After some fumbled sentences, her father mentioned what a "rotter" of a Prime Minister Blair was, to involve Britain in this war. Everyone sat silent for a while. Philippa's mother stood, they all did, and she said, "We'll have more to say at dinner." She smiled gently at him and he felt encouraged to try one of Nigel's phrases. "Right, see you in a bit." She blinked, paused, and said, "Yes, we'll see you shortly," and then turned away.

An uncomfortable day passed, but then the flirting started, a few good-humored insults that turned into something kind of romantic. He got the feeling that Philippa was grabbing and holding on to her brother through him. But why be bothered by that? A few times in his life he'd imagined he was in love, but it hadn't had the same impact. Within a day or two everyone in the house had detected what was going on. He knew her parents didn't think he was right for her, but they were used to their spoiled daughter's screw-you choices. Because *she* didn't care, he didn't.

Pippa's uncle rode over from his place across the river. Because he was something of a star in the family, a military hero and former MP, everyone had gone downstairs and out onto the gravel to greet him. He trotted up in smart but old riding clothes, flipped his right leg over the skewbald mare's neck, and dropped lightly to its left side. After planting a peck on everyone's cheek, he turned toward Mark and looked him over during Pippa's minimal introduction. Only the wounded leg seemed to make any impression. He asked about it when Mark limped back into the house. You got the feeling that in his book, a wounded soldier's drawbacks could be ignored; or should be.

Maybe Pippa's parents saw things the same way. They didn't object when she announced the engagement. If a weird marriage was a disappointment, it didn't compare to the loss of their boy, and you sensed that something pessimistic had settled over the family and taken all the fight out of them. Maybe it had begun even earlier, when Nigel told them not to expect him to marry, which meant that their cousins would have to carry on the family name. Pippa hadn't been in a rush to marry, too, so the prospect of a grandchild with any name at all might have struck them as better than nothing. Pippa's mother absorbed the news with a simple smile as she whisked aside a lock of brown and gray hair with the back of her right hand.

The little church attached to the estate was filled for their wedding, and some people had come up from London, but you couldn't call it a big, fancy-pants bash. Maybe a honeymoon in Connemara in the West Country of Ireland wouldn't be most people's first choice, but he'd never been there and thought it was beautiful, to the extent he and Pippa ever got out of their room in the hotel. He would look at her hair, spread out on the pillow like a fistful of copper wire and think, I always wanted a redhead. But she got angry when he said it.

"You realize I'm not just a head of hair."

"I know, but you never mind when I say the dress you're wearing is pretty, and it's not even attached to your body."

"Right, but I choose my clothes whereas I didn't choose my hair."

"Some people dye theirs."

"They do. I hope you know that if it had been dark, I wouldn't have colored mine red just for you."

He touched her. "You sure about that?"

A giggle and then, "Well. Maybe on holiday." She stroked his face. "As long as we're on physical features, you know, you've got pretty much the same nose that Nige had. You could be our distant American cousin, what do you think?"

It came to him that he'd never been truly happy, or only at a few points earlier in his life, like on those hunting and camping trips with the one foster dad who'd paid any attention to him. Too much attention, as it later turned out. When he was finally old enough to decide for himself, it felt like he just had to get through the rest of his life the best way he could. The military was part of the solution. You gave your service, and if you got your chips cashed in, too bad. At least nobody could say you were an asshole.

He had to go back, the duty (dirty) tour wasn't finished with him yet, he was to report in two days' time. During one of his wrap-it-up conversations, Mark jobbed in another of Nigel's phrases, something he'd popped out with as he saluted and set out for his mission: "Once more into the breach!" Even if the exact meaning wasn't clear, it fit, one more spare part in Nigel's way of asserting his identity. It fit his ironic expression, his curly black hair, his green eyes. Funny how Nigel, even though dead, was still around tweaking whatever happened. Pippa accepted that Mark's return to Helmand Province was mandatory but said, "Be sure you get me pregnant before you go."

"What, as an insurance policy if I end up dead?"

"Nigel didn't come back, and we were all sure he would. We Bourchiers were always a practical lot."

"I'm kind of practical-minded too. I'm doing my best to get you there." He gave her his bad boy look, the one she liked.

They didn't know whether he'd succeeded or not by the time he left, but eventually news came that his cue stick had scored and that they'd put one in the corner pocket. The thought made him dizzy, which was dangerous because you have to stay focused. None of Talibanistan had ever seemed like it was really there even before the move to this new terrain, the ten-mile stretches of reddish-tan sand with gray-green scrub, where you wore camo that was supposed to hide you and didn't, much. Everything was out in the open, not a tree in sight. You'd be rumbling down the road in the Bearcat and have no trouble seeing men sprawled on their bellies as they aimed a Barrett at nothing special, their legs vee'd out behind them, or walking around in helmets like aliens, with both arms holding their rifles pointed at the ground. But now, after Pippa's news, it was even less real, all of it. Like they say: the love-story side of life really fucks up the military. It was already fucked up anyway, as he had realized the day he watched those big planes that used to come from New Hampshire to fuel the jets and now were refitted for a different cargo: the coffins to be shipped back to the surviving family, each one with a flag draped over them as a cover-up. And he'd see news broadcasts where some amazingly stupid Pentagon brass would say the "nuclear option" wasn't off the table.

It came to him a long time ago that Lady Luck didn't much like him, Pippa being the big exception to the rule. Well, and the fact that he'd come through whereas Nigel hadn't. But then the roulette wheel spun again. Pippa had the crazy idea their kid (like Bruce Springsteen) should be born in the USA. It was a nod to the father's nationality. From the practical standpoint, it would be so much easier for the child to register for citizenship if that later turned out to be important. After all, Mark still hadn't qualified for his UK passport. So, when the baby was just beginning to show, she booked a flight to New York, where it turned out she had as she said "many dear friends." The bulk of the trip would be spent in New York, but one of her friends had a country place near Mount Washington in New Hampshire, so that was also part of the plan.

He heard what had happened while he was still recovering in the field hospital. Another wound to the leg, the same one, which was good luck or bad, depending on how you felt about it. The message said that there was a difficult breech birth, after which the infant had been stillborn; that the mother had contracted a MRSA infection and in her weakened condition hadn't survived. Through an oxycontin haze he found himself mouthing the phrase, "There are no words," but he didn't say them aloud. Because there weren't any, not even those.

As soon as his discharge came through, he went to Belfort Hall. Her parents didn't have words, either. They and Pippa's uncle sat in the drawing room and expressed sympathy for his ruined leg. Pippa's mother started to say something about his being demobilized but then revised her sentence into, "They won't ask you to return to combat, will they." Her husband turned to her, then back to him and opened his mouth to speak before shutting it again. Mark imagined he saw an extra streak of white in the thick gray hair and wondered if the half-squint of his eyes had been there before, just not noticed until now. Pippa's mother then reached for an envelope placed on the big ottoman between them and held it out, murmuring that something had come for him while he was away. His passport. He stared at the red cover, looked up and thanked her. He guessed they had pulled strings to speed up the process. But what was he supposed to do with it? She said, "You must stay with us as long as you like. We couldn't be more pleased if you would."

As long as you like. He looked at the paintings, the furniture, the Oriental vases, the silver-framed family photographs on the piano and felt pressure from it all, pressure to leave. He'd come thousands of miles to get here, too long a distance for it to make sense to stay. What kind of chores would he do to be helpful around the house? Replace the blown fuses? Mow the lawn, all five acres of it? Push one or both wheelchairs when the day came? Uh, no. They all walked over to the churchyard attached to the little chapel where the wedding had happened. There was a nice headstone, but somehow, he hadn't prepared himself to see his own name on it, recording Pippa's married name. Grass had been seeded over the mound of dirt in front of it but wasn't grown yet. Underneath, that's where Pippa was. Well, not really. She wasn't anywhere now. And no grandchild for her parents. Nothing.

Where he decided to stay was London, at least for a while. He found a tiny single room with bath, fridge and two burners in a cheap residence hotel in Belsize Park. An old building, its three floors filled with rooms. They gave you sheets but no towels, so he bought a couple at a discount place. Walls were thin. If there were people in the next room, you heard their conversation. Yes, but without understanding anything because it was usually being carried on in another language. Still, the international language of laughter could be understood, even though people from different countries laugh differently. The Bulgarian he met in the hall was kind of addicted to laughing. His style was to start low and then zoom up high, rapidly repeating the same note for a few seconds—*he-he-he-he-he*—before breaking off.

The routine was the same for nearly every day except Sunday, when nothing was open. He'd have his two eggs, toast and coffee, watch the news for a while, and then, picking up his crutch, make his way down one flight, ignoring stabs of pain along the way. Belsize Avenue slopes upward as you go toward Haverstock Hill, so he didn't walk fast. But eventually he'd get there and turn in the direction of the supermarket.

The return trip was easier just from the fact it went downhill, but he had to manage a couple bags of food, which always banged against the crutch in the rhythm of his steps. The best way to avoid pain was to stretch out on the bed, but a day or two of that and you were ready for the dudes in white coats.

He sometimes had enough get-up-and-go to make sight-seeing trips. Hampstead was close, and you could even get to the Heath without too much trouble. On the days when he felt especially ambitious, he'd get on a bus and just ride down into the center city. It was too awkward to climb the stairs to the upper level of the bus, but even on the lower, you could see a lot. He didn't try to find out exactly what it all was, he just looked at everything like a picture. Pippa could have named the buildings and told him who the statues represented if she'd been there. Now, the way things stood, he could feel the hole inside his mind where she used to be. Buses made no effort to be convenient, and if you missed one you had a fifteen-minute wait. How many times did the doors close and the big red vehicle pull away from the curb just as he was hobbling toward the door. At least then there would be an empty seat to sit on for those fifteen minutes, a cold seat made of metal meshwork. The bus stop at the intersection of Belsize Avenue and Haverstock stood opposite a store front that had once been a "Quik-Cleaners," now closed. Its plate-glass windows were covered on the inside with old newspapers, and his long sit-down there gave him time to see that they were from *The Camden Journal*, whose headlines he could read, though not the articles. One time, just to relieve boredom, he got up and moved close enough to see what they said. The word "Love" printed over a picture of a sofa in a furniture sale. Articles about crime in Camden Town. And a cheery feature about a party one of the churches gave for returning vets.

On a day of unusual determination, he got as far as St. Paul's Cathedral. That building, he recognized. He stood on the steps for a while looking up at the columns flanking the entrance. For him, if you got religion, you were pretty much admitting defeat, showing you couldn't take care of yourself. That was why he wasn't going to go in. He turned around and saw a big stone monument surrounded by a white-painted iron fence. He stumbled over the pavement in that direction, noticing two pretty girls looking down at a book and then up at the statue on top of the thing. A woman in flowing robes, her right hand holding a stick pointing down toward the spectators. Closer in, he saw she was holding a ball in her left hand. Also, she wore a little crown. One of the girls said, "It's Queen Anne. I think she came much later than Queen Elizabeth." From her accent he could tell the girl was American—or maybe Canadian, but anyway not British. He looked up at the statue. No resemblance to Pippa. The wand pointing down reminded him of the way soldiers always held their rifles pointed down. One of the girls saw him and, noticing the crutch, gave him a serious look, the wrinkles in her forehead then relaxing quickly as soon as she smiled. Though it hurt, he smiled back. Damn, a redhead. He must have stared too long because she turned aside and whispered something to her friend, just before they walked away.

Queen Anne was dead. Dead, dead. Most of the people alive today were halfway dead, if you want to know the truth. The flag-covered coffins keep coming from assorted combat zones, crossing the water to where half-dead people wait for them. Death was spreading over the world like a nuclear cloud. He was halfway a stiff himself, and getting deader all the time. OK. OK. Time to go back home. Get himself cleaned up to look like a soldier again, instead of this unshaven bum thing he'd let himself slip into. Maybe once back in the States he could get the dead half of him operating at full function. Or near to being. He'd take the UK passport with him because it came from Pippa. Since it was hers, he didn't care that the picture of him in it was plug-ugly. She'd never thought he was ugly. She had wanted his kid and died trying to have it.

PROVIDENCE

She poured water from the saucepan, bubbling boiling water, noticing how it began spitting when it slid over heated metal before sluicing into the teapot. Sharp hot pinpricks hit her hand, stinging but not serious. While the tea was brewing, she went back to where Herman's clothes were piled on the dark green sofa. The task at hand was to sort through his shirts and jackets. She'd needed a year after he died to begin dealing with them. Each one was connected to a memory. For instance, his favorite sport coat, a herringbone tweed, which he used to wear when they went on leaf-peeping trips up to Vermont. Or this blue blazer, the very last one he wore before the end. She held it to her face for a quick sniff. Nothing of him, instead, a faint naptha smell, and Herman didn't like mothballs. Again, the pang intermittently felt during the last twelve months.

She was going to have to drink the tea quickly and take the clothes to Providence's Salvation Army because Kevin was coming to cut the grass at 2:00. Not that she liked the Salvation Army, an institution she thought of as exploitative. But it was either take the clothes there or throw them out, and that idea—well, no. She gathered up an armful and left the house for the short trip down to the S.A. It had taken her a while to get used to driving everywhere since Herman had always been in charge of transportation. Nowadays she seldom took the car out of the East Side, but she was fine doing little errands within a radius of a couple of miles.

Putting out of mind the unwelcome idea of a fake Santa Claus ringing a bell next to a red metal pot, she pushed through the doors of the Army. The clerk at the counter said, "Oh, Mrs. Greene, how're you. Brought us something today? Men's clothes, it looks like, very nice." They always called her Mrs. Greene, though she'd told them her name was Maddie Greene. The clerk went through the usual formalities but "Mrs. Greene" didn't accept the receipt, even though she knew some people use that in their tax returns as a charitable deduction. Coincidence: turning away from the counter she saw someone in line to buy an armful of shirts he held on his arm. A thought came to her: she wondered who would end up with Herman's shirts and coats. It might not be someone nice, and she didn't know how she felt about that. But then it was easy to imagine Herman saying it didn't matter in the least: whoever needed or wanted them should have them. And of course he would be right. Task done, she left the building.

Lunch consisted of a little green salad and a pickled matjes herring, with a handful of organic blueberries for dessert. The herring was a taste she'd acquired from Herman. Before their marriage she'd never had it. He said it was a Hungarian specialty, a little hard to find outside New York, where he'd grown up. But he'd persuaded Whole Foods to stock it, and they continued to do so even now that he… was no longer the person buying it, but instead she. When people marry, they always acquire tastes and habits from each other. Her idea was that she'd acquired more from Herman than he had from her; though Herman might have said the opposite.

She took her exercise walk, a turn onto Wayland and then onto Orchard Street. As on every other day, she passed a big brick house behind a high brick wall built maybe a hundred years ago. The owners had also gone to the trouble (maintaining uniformity) of laying down a brick-paved sidewalk out front. Tree roots below the bricks over the years swelled and lifted the bricks' reddish-brown herringbone pattern as though a wave of earth had moved under them and then frozen. It was a good idea to step carefully until the brickwork gave way to normal paving. Farther on there was St. Martin's Episcopal and next to it the Beth El synagogue. In her mind the two buildings summarized her marriage: she, Christian, Herman Jewish. When people said that

Herman didn't look Jewish, as for some reason or other they often rudely did, she would answer, "I don't look Christian, either, do I?" Because in fact not all WASPs are Christians, you know. Nevertheless, she had peeped into St. Martin's one Good Friday, discovering that the congregation was in the process of doing the Stations of the Cross. That didn't appeal to her much, so she left. She supposed that she wasn't a very good Christian anyway and had even considered converting to Judaism, but then Herman wasn't especially religious himself, so it didn't make much sense to do it. They both believed in leading ethical lives, which ought to be enough for most purposes.

Home again. The house on Adelphi didn't have much grass, and she was pretty sure this would be the last time it was cut before winter snows covered everything. Kevin arrived, this time wearing long pants rather than shorts because weather had already turned cool. Also, a green bandanna tied around his neck to soak up sweat. He said hello but not much else and turned away to unload the lawnmower from his van. She'd never been sure whether he liked her, he was so reserved. That hadn't been her experience with other Chinese-Americans, but then Kevin had been born in Vietnam, brought here by his parents when he was still an infant, which might explain the difference. Before meeting him, she hadn't known that there'd been, long before the Vietnam war, a large Chinese community in Saigon. Christians, most of them, and probably better at it than she was. Kevin (his American name) was tall, nice-looking, and strong, but she didn't want to think of him as attractive because he was only twenty-five. Partly deaf from a childhood illness, he didn't like wearing his hearing aid, she gathered, a fact that probably explained his reserve. She often had to repeat what she said, which seemed to annoy him even more than it did her. He wasn't married, and when she asked if he might be dating anyone, he shook his head, almost as if the question was rude. Well, she knew it wasn't easy being a minority in America, no matter what people claimed. And then his deafness. On the off chance that their two medical problems would establish a bond, she'd considered telling him about her own macular degeneration, an impairment in seeing that was only going to get worse every year. It had started as just a black pinprick at the center of her vision, like the period at the end of a sentence, so small she didn't pay much attention to it. Until the dot began to get bigger. Several times she was on the point of mentioning her condition to Kevin but was afraid he might take it the wrong way, so she left things as they were.

The lawn took less than half an hour to mow. She'd given Kevin his $20.00 even before he began, so there was no surprise if he left without saying goodbye. Maybe that was a little inconsiderate, but other people are different from us, there was no reason to disapprove. She checked to see if the lawn looked all right, and, as always, Kevin had done a good job. Going up the steps to the door, she noticed he'd left his bandanna on the stoop. She picked it up, a little gingerly, then called him on the phone. He said he had several other lawns to take care of that afternoon and asked if he could drop by around five. He did want his bandanna back. She suggested they meet in the little park on Humboldt, did he know the one? He did. It was part of her routine to walk there in the late afternoon when the weather was fine.

Meanwhile, she had an hour of desk work to do, bill-paying, to be precise: she'd never learned how to remit online. A certain pleasing tedium went with the task. She had to write checks and slip them into the provided envelope, then affix a stamp with a firm thumb, taking a sip of tea between each bill handled. Herman used to take care of it all, so she always felt a little heavy-hearted when bill-paying time came. When you've loved, everything reminds you of the person. Around the room, for example, were the Chinese export porcelains Herman collected, partly because he'd inherited a few from his mother but then got interested in collecting others. She'd once invited Kevin in to have a look, but she quickly saw he didn't make much of them and maybe thought she was pigeonholing him as Oriental when he was in fact more American than anything else. She liked the porcelains partly because Herman did. This one, for example, a pattern known as "Nanking," in blue and white, like the "Blueplate" dishes diners used to serve meals on. There were crudely drawn mountains at the top, a stone bridge at the bottom, and a pagoda on the right next to a Chinese-type tree. Through the window of the pagoda, you could see a solitary Chinese man in profile, sitting motionless, probably reading. All by himself. The black dot in her eyes partly obscured his image. Dear man. The hairs on her forearms prickled. Then silly tears. The plate went back to its place on the shelf.

Administrative chores completed, she opened a notebook where she'd been sketching out ideas that might be used for a special project that had been on the back burner for a while. For nearly a year she'd been plotting to get an appearance on *Stories from the Stage*, a PBS program out of Boston in which ordinary folks got up in front of an audience and told interesting anecdotes about something they'd been through in their lives. It looked like so much fun. Years ago, she'd volunteered at the public library to read stories to preschoolers, a job she enjoyed. But then the library terminated the program, citing lack of funds. It seems you have to take out liability insurance for kids involved in special activities. She missed seeing the children every week. At first, she thought she could never be chosen for *Stories from the Stage*, considering she was just a senior widow who lived in Rhode Island, not an especially exciting category. But then she saw a woman from Boston (also up in years) stand and speak boldly into the mic and get a lot of applause. So, there was really no excuse not to try. Every human life counts for something, surely, even if it wasn't heroic. Something her mother (a rather old-school person born and raised in Litchfield, Connecticut) used to say: "Every station in life, humble or high-placed, deserves respect if the person in question lives it decently." No arguing with that. The main problem was, for this program you had to have a good story. She'd been sketching out various possibilities but hadn't hit on one that was interesting enough. The story needed a surprise near the end, maybe a startling coincidence that made sense of all the earlier details. There had to be some sort of click, the needle you'd been searching for in the haystack. None of the anecdotes she occasionally told at friends' dinner parties seemed original enough.

Still, discouragement hadn't won out yet, maybe because of something that had happened a couple of winters back. About a month after Christmas, a snowstorm had hit Providence in the early evening, and on a whim Herman had proposed that they go for a little walk to enjoy it. (He often had these unusual ideas, not all of them practical.) They went out into a light fall of powder snow, icy pinpricks blowing into their faces as their boots crunched along sidewalks that hadn't yet been shoveled. They turned off Wayland onto Orchard and noticed warm lights at various windows. One house still had a lit-up Christmas tree in the front room. You shouldn't keep a tree up that long, but she knew that for many people Christmas decorations were connected to happy memories they didn't want to let go of until forced to. Herman hadn't noticed the Christmas tree, so she pointed it out with a little laugh. "They want Santa to keep showing up," he said. "Santa's become lot more popular than the babe in the manger, who never had a Christmas tree as far as I know. But then he was also spared the disappointment of being told that Santa was just a story." They laughed together. She was glad they'd made their excursion out into the snow, walking along, exchanging anecdotes. It occurred to her that you never enjoyed something 100 percent unless it was shared with somebody else. Living your life in the fullest way meant telling it to others. Except that she didn't have anyone who would care to listen now, Mother and Father gone, her sister not speaking to her since their disagreement about their parents' estate. Of course you can remember good moments just by yourself, but that wasn't quite enough. Conveying how you felt about some part of your life to others, as though it was a meal you had prepared, that was what she wanted to do with *Stories from the Stage*. Question was, which incident from her life deserved to be told?

The events around Herman's passing were dramatic but probably too gloomy, lacking the essential ingredient of a happy ending. He'd taken Amtrak down to New York to meet with his financial adviser, an overnight trip there was no reason for her to make with him. After the call came, though, she had to hurry down herself to join him at Bellevue Hospital. Once there, she spoke to a Dr. Li, who reported that Herman's condition was serious, but that there was every reason to hope for a good outcome. Going down subway steps he'd slipped and fallen. Broken bones might not have been grave, but the fall had brought on a cardiac event. Total shock. She had never been so afraid in her life.

When Herman finally woke up, she went to the bedside and took his hand. He was confused, mumbling words in no special order, and she had trouble understanding. Not much of it made sense. Eventually he became more coherent and asked if they had taken contact information from the man.

"What man do you mean?"

"The one that helped me. He called 911."

"Oh. Nobody told me that. Who was he?"

"I don't know, I was hoping they got a telephone number. He folded his jacket and put it under my head while we were waiting for them to come."

"Oh. That was thoughtful. What did he look like?"

"Can't quite remember. A little younger than me. Brown hair, eyeglasses. I want to thank him. He talked to me so that I wouldn't be anxious."

"I'll ask later. Don't worry about it now." (In retrospect, she would wish that the conversation had been more meaningful, more heartfelt.)

She did later ask people in charge about "the man" but drew a complete blank. No one knew about him, and the question was, had Herman dreamed it? Entirely possible, she thought, when Dr. Li told her they'd discovered a concussion. That meant a longer hospital stay. Hearing the news, she felt a wave of nausea, which must somehow be brought under control. She also had to find a hotel. After only one night, though, it happened: another cardiac event, this one final. She didn't permit herself to break down because there was so much to do, a hundred arrangements to make. Collapse and suchlike would have to wait. In fact, they were kept in abeyance until after Herman was safely at rest in Swan Point Cemetery, where several years earlier he'd had the foresight to get a plot. One brother who now lived in Japan came for the funeral and one cousin from Atlanta. Her own sister didn't come, nor was the bereavement voicemail message ever answered. How could anyone be that bitter? There's no reasoning with people. They go to extremes, too selfish or too unselfish. Revisiting her last conversation with Herman, she decided that it *was* meaningful, it *was* heartfelt. Herman had shown again that his concern was for others. He'd wanted to thank the man who'd helped him in an hour of need. It was like Herman to feel that way, even in a hospital bed. One more reason to love him.

She put aside her notebook and checked the time. She should go over to the park now to meet Kevin. She slipped the green bandanna into her coat pocket and went downstairs. Up Wayland again but this time as far as Humboldt and on to the little park and playground there. Fall foliage, sunlight on the children's play structure and the swings. The bench behind the swings was empty, the perfect place to sit down, now that she was a little out of breath. All the swings were taken: preschoolers safely held in leather-strap bucket seats. Some of the mothers (no fathers present) pushed from behind, and a smaller number faced their kids as they pushed, which was harder to do, it seemed. Back and forth, with an occasional little wail from one of the kids. For the ten-thousandth time she brushed aside the wish that there had been children for Herman and herself. Someone to talk to now, even if just by telephone. She found her handkerchief and applied it to her eyes. Back and forth in the autumn sunlight, upswing, downswing. It wasn't all that easy to ignore the black dot that hovered in front of everything she focused on.

Who? She looked up as the man approached, tall, a little younger, and rather nice-looking, professorial maybe in his horn-rimmed glasses. "Afternoon. Mind if I sit here?"

"Not at all." There was more confidence in that phrase than in her actual feeling. A brief smile served as a cover for rapid appraisal. Graying beard, blue-gray eyes crinkled at the corners. Jacket in brown and green tweed.

"I'm Al." Said with a subdued chuckle, the kind that makes you return it with something more than the standard brushoff.

"And I'm Maddie." A pause. "I don't recall seeing you here before."

"I'm not from Providence. I was here attending a conference at Brown University. Just came from lunch with colleagues at one of the restaurants over on Angell."

"You're a professor of—?"

"Parasitology."

An answer both impressive and distancing. "That's an unusual field. How did you come to choose it?"

Another chuckle. "I think it was because I once had a parasite myself."

They were straying into too-much-information territory, but she pushed on. "Oh. How did that happen?"

"When I was a kid—this was in South Georgia, during a visit to my aunt and uncle's farm out in the country. It was summer so I went around barefoot. Picked up hookworm. We town folks didn't even know what that was. Pretty easy to cure, but anyway it got me interested in the whole subject."

"I guess I have to admit I've never heard of it either. I associate parasites with third-world—I mean, developing countries. My sister's son, when he came back from Vietnam, had a kind of amoeba parasite."

"Coincidence: that was the first parasite I researched."

She was beginning to feel empathetic and said, "Small world. I like coincidences."

"You do? Why is that?"

"I don't know. The way things fall into place and make a meaning, even if you can't quite say what it is." He nodded, but she wasn't sure he understood.

Then he said, "Do you know about Alcoholics Anonymous?"

That came as a surprise. "Yes, I do. Why? I'm not a member of it, though."

"No, I'm sure you're not. But I am."

Another surprise. "Really? You don't look—." She caught herself in time.

He laughed. "Members look all kinds of ways. Anyhow, I'm going to quote a saying we have in A.A."

"A saying?"

"Yes. 'Coincidence is the Higher Power's way of maintaining his anonymity.' The term Higher Power is what we, some of us, call God."

"Maintaining his anonymity. I see." But she wasn't altogether sure she did. "You mean … you're saying he works behind the scenes, so to speak."

"Something like that. If it is in fact a he."

Things were getting complicated, so she changed the subject. "So then do you spend most of your time in the classroom or in medical labs?"

"More teaching than research now. Sometimes I visit hospitals."

"Oh, that's always so depressing."

"Is it? Because, you know, the patients are getting the help they need to recover."

"If they do recover.... Of course, you're right. It's just that—I hope you don't mind—my husband died in hospital a little over a year ago. Down in New York."

"I'm sorry. I live in New York. Which hospital was it?"

"Bellevue."

"Know it well." Silence. "You were living in New York then?"

"No. He'd gone down by himself on business. His heart ... he had a cardiac event. In a subway station, if you can imagine. He fell down the stairs." She wished she hadn't gone this far, it all just tumbled out. And to a perfect stranger. She looked at her hands, lying palms upward in her lap.

"In the subway? Do you know which station?" There was an odd tension in his voice.

"Lexington Avenue and 53rd Street."

"Oh, yes? This was about a year ago?" A forlorn nod. "I ... I'm sorry, but I'm wondering ... you see, September year ago, I helped a man who ... had a fall in the subway. That was the station. I believe it was his heart."

She stared. "Can you describe him?"

"Well, roughly my age, perhaps a little older. Glasses. A blue blazer, white shirt, but no tie."

The shock she felt registered in his face. He said, "I'm terribly sorry. I hope I haven't—."

They gradually pieced together the details. She hardly knew what she was saying but explained that Herman had wanted to thank him. Had wanted that so very much. She *had* tried to find out who the Good Samaritan was, obviously without success. Now it was hard to believe that here in Providence—. Would he please join her for dinner? Unfortunately, no. Or a cup of tea? He regretted that he had an Amtrak train to catch shortly and had just been killing time—that is, filling it— by having a stroll in this neighborhood. She had seldom felt so awkward as now, and it came as an alleviating distraction when she saw Kevin walking up. After a minimal introduction, man and boy shook hands. Kevin looked suspicious, mistrustful, seeing her with someone he didn't know. It struck her that the boy in some way or other was assuming a protective role with her. That he wanted to make sure the man wasn't any kind of risk. It was touching. She hadn't known she particularly mattered to Kevin, he'd never shown that before. She reached into her pocket and handed him his bandanna, which she thanked her for.

The conversation that followed was made up of dull irrelevancies, useful even so in that it dispensed her from the effort to process in all its depth the information she'd received, all the while maintaining a sociable façade. Kevin seemed to be reassured that the man was OK, no threat to her. He must have put in his hearing aid because he didn't ask either of them to repeat their sentences and understood everything that was said. The man—Al, rather—gave her his card and agreed they should be in touch. Then said he'd better call his Uber; he had his train to catch.

Kevin surprised her by asking, "Is that Amtrak? I'm going past the station on my way home and could take you, if you want to." They looked at each other.

"Well, um, sure, thank you, if it's no trouble." They gazed at each other, a smile breaking out on both faces. Some sort of wordless exchange was going on. Odd.

To break the silence, she said, "Oh, that's convenient. Goodness. Thank you, Kevin, if you're sure it's not out of your way." He shook his head. Goodbyes, as cordial as it's possible to make them among strangers; and then the two strolled off together. She watched them leave the park. In what looked like a perfectly natural gesture, the man—Al, she should call him—reached behind and put his hand on Kevin's shoulder. Oh. *That* was it. Everything came clear. She felt silly and unobservant for never having realized that Kevin was … you know.

Good for him. She wondered if he and the man—Al—would become friends. That would be nice, she thought.

She turned back to the swings. One father had brought his kid into the park in a little wheeled vehicle shaped like a swan. He pulled the little boy out of it and found a swing for him among the others already in motion. One Dad among all the Moms, that was nice. Up and down, back and forth. Red leaves and sunlight went liquid, the swings' motion now seen through a pane of wavering saltwater. Plus, the pinprick of the black dot. But these weren't tears of sadness, finally. The simplicity of it made her feel that a high brick wall between her and who she truly was had crumbled, collapsed, fallen; so that loveliness rose in her like an ocean wave. She didn't know the names of the children or their mothers' names. But in a very strange way, they were hers, the little children in their autumn coats and knit caps; and so, Herman's too. Well, not really, of course. Not really. But she'd find a way to put them into the story she wanted to tell on the program.

Acknowledgements

Grateful acknowledgment is made to the magazines and anthologies where these stories appeared: *Ontario Review; Cutthroat; Ganymede; Harrington's Gay Men's Fiction; Molly House; Speak My Language; Like Light: 25 Years of Poetry & Prose by Bright Hill Poets and Writers.*

About the Author

ALFRED CORN has published eleven books of poetry, the most recent a selected poems volume titled *The Returns* (2022). His novels are *Part of His Story* and *Miranda's Book*. Three collections of his essays have appeared: *The Metamorphoses of Metaphor*, *Atlas: Selected Essays: 1989–2007*, and *Arks & Covenants*. He has received the Guggenheim, the NEA, an Award in Literature from the Academy of Arts and Letters, and one from the Academy of American Poets. He received the Premio Andersen, offered in 2014 by the Comune di Sestri Levante, Italy, for a wonder tale titled "The Lost Wings." His teaching experience includes courses in creative writing at Yale, Columbia, the University of Cincinnati, and UCLA. In 2013 he was made a Life Fellow of Clare Hall, Cambridge. In the spring of 2016 Chamán Ediciones in Spain published *Rocinante*, a selection of his work translated in Spanish, the same translation appearing the following year in Mexico under the title *Antonio en el desierto*. In 2017 Corn was inducted into the Georgia Writers' Hall of Fame. In 2021 Norton published his translation of Rilke's *Duino Elegies*. A selection of his poems translated into Italian appeared in 2024 with I Quaderni del Bardo under the title *Tutto ciò che è*. *Hosts* is his first collection of short stories.

www.ingramcontent.com/pod-product-compliance
Lightning Source LLC
Chambersburg PA
CBHW032007010726

47493CB00007B/2314